The Defenders

Reita O'Neal Jackson

Published by Hickory Hill, 2023.

THE DEFENDERS

First edition. October 15, 2023.

Copyright © 2023 Reita O'Neal Jackson.

ISBN: 979-8223916925

Written by Reita O'Neal Jackson.

For Nate, a constant marvel with an incredible imagination. Thanks for help in naming some of my characters, and for inspiring me every day.

Terrene

Longer ago than anyone can remember, a primordial forest stood sentinel over the massive, forgotten island of Terrene, which protrudes like a mighty ship of enormous proportions from the choppy waters of the Sea of Mists.

When you think about it, it's quite easy to imagine why this land might have been lost to time. The dense, unabating mists which gave the sea its name, shrouded the island in a cloak of invisibility. Wary seamen were hesitant to risk their ships or their crews by traveling blind into this hidden realm.

Even if the seaworthiest of ships somehow managed to blunder through the perilous mists, they would find only turbulent, unrelenting waters that could easily dash a ship to bits in a matter of minutes. If by some very unlikely chance, a courageous and wise sea captain somehow made his way through the waters, he would find steep, impenetrable mountains that formed the outer perimeter of the island barring him from landing.

As eons passed and this secret world was remade a thousand times over, the giant mountains grew ever taller. The vast ancient forest withstood the test of time, its massive trees reaching always towards the light.

As time continued to pass, changes were inevitable, and so it was with Terrene. Storms, lightning strikes, wind, drought, ever-changing temperatures, erosion, and much more played their parts. The land became more diverse, with flowing grasslands, deep valleys, steep mountains, magical woodlands, and rivers traversing it from mountain range to mountain range.

Then, almost as though they fell from the sky, creatures of every ilk began to make their home on Terrene. Your guess is as good as mine as to how they got there, but there they were, nonetheless. Elves, fairies, piskies, gnomes, fearsome wolves, giant eagles, mighty dragons, canny warrior insects, and the wizard dragon master himself.

And after many, many more years had gone by, humans appeared. Only a few at first, but over the years there were more, and more, and more. Still, for all that, the island remained sparsely populated and peaceful by most measures, until evil entered stealthily one day and threatened the island and its inhabitants with annihilation.

Prologue

Kamahi trees begin life by twining onto other trees. This creates a gnarled and contorted forest that is home to isnanas, the hideous giant spiders that live in the northwestern section of the Kamahi Forest, and to piskies, pesky small creatures that inhabit the eastern part of the forest. Men rarely venture here, afraid they will be caught in the twisting, tenacious vines and massive briar patches that loop and grasp their way over the crooked, gruesome trees. It is an eerie, foreboding place for the most part, even more so because in the isnana land the River of Death flows through the grisly forest, fooling any passerby that unwittingly stumbles alongside it into believing that its gently flowing rainbow colored waters are safe. Its shallow, seemingly calm waters lure you in - but travelers beware! Once you are in the water, the current strengthens until you are swept swiftly along, unable to return to shore. When the unwary soul reaches the hidden waterfalls it is too late, for careless travelers are plunged into an abyss. If the abyss doesn't get them, which it most likely will, the bottomless whirlpools will drag them to their doom.

The small river that flows lazily through the piskies' land is called the Sapphire River, and the Ceffyl Dwr call this river home. They are water horses that can evaporate into mist and can also fly. The piskies' land is not so treacherous as the land of the isnanas. In fact, it is a breathtaking, enchanting land.

The Blue Forest sits south of the Kamahi and stretches across a swath of land along the western Crystal Mountains. Blues of every hue sparkle across the floor of the forest. The colors are intense and endless, unbroken by boulders, fallen trees, or grassy interlopers. The Blue River meanders crookedly along the center of the forest floor, feeding the Sapphire River that flows northward into the Kamahi land. It appears deep blue, but if you were to dip your cup into the cold water, you would find the water clear. Its looks deceive because of the reflections of the blue flora surrounding it.

Otherwise, the only things marring the blue carpet are the skinny trees with their blue tinged leaves that bend toward the center of the forest and rise to meet the cerulean sky above, and a tiny path that curves through the forest, barely wide enough for a man's foot to tread upon. The Crystal Mountains lie to the west and are home to blue gnomes.

South of the Blue Forest and north of Fearann Draoidh, or Wizard's Domain, lies a wood of limited acreage. Mossy boulders lay in heaps, some like stairsteps; others a tumbled mass – as if a giant hand had thrown them into disarray. The wood is within the mountain where a giant cavern toppled in, allowing light to filter into the wood and to bathe the wizard's garden in sunlight.

Trees as old as the world stand hunched and stunted by the boulders that lay strewn across their roots. The ancient relics speak of druids, hauntings, and mythical creatures. It is thought that venomous snakes must surely lie in wait among the boulders, ready to strike at a moment's notice. It must be said, however, that no one can attest to this belief. In one place the trees form loops, rings, and even heart shapes. It is a magical place.

Most of the wood is filled with wildlife. Trees bear ample quantities of fruit. Wild herbs grow profusely in the tiny meadows within the wood. Underground springs feed a creek that runs from the Crystal Mountains through the wood and into the Fearann Draoidh Mountain. Here it disappears, retreating underground. This creek is teeming with bream, perch, trout, and crawfish.

A riot of mushrooms grows in the damp grounds near the stream and in the deep wood. Wild onions, dandelions, wood sorrel, and watercress thrive. Plump berries hang in profusion from vines and bushes. Perhaps not quite as appetizing, but nutritional all the same, are the various tree roots, bark, and edible leaves.

A worn path that begins at Grayson's garden (we will get to him in a moment) meanders through the wood and ends abruptly at a tumbled mass of boulders a mile or more from Fingal's Land.

The Great Southern Plains are bordered by the Fearann Draoidh Mountain and Fingal's Land on the west and north, the Misty Mountains on the east, and the Cagar Mountains to the south.

The summers are warm and humid in the Plains, and the winters are cool and dry. Rainfall averages twenty-five inches per year. Trees do not grow in this temperate environment, but the perennial grasses flourish. The soil is rich and almost black due to calcification.

Animals such as squirrels, antelopes, ferrets, coyotes, rabbits, and an occasional wild horse visit the Plains, but do not call it home. They live in the forests or low on the sides of the mountain. Phantom cats - massive, invisible panthers called Specters - call the Plains their home. Other animals enter the Plains at their peril. They cannot see or smell the Specters until it is too late. Thankfully, the big cats do not need to eat but every few weeks.

The Gehenna land is stunning, but treacherous. It lies east of the Great Southern Plains and Fingal's Land, north of the Valley of the Forgotten Abbey, and south of the Land of Frozen Waters. The colors are phenomenal and vivid – red, blue, yellow, green, orange, purple, and brown. Look closely, though. Savvy travelers do not allow themselves to be mesmerized by the beauty of this land, but those who are not quite so cautious; well, that is another story.

A thin, smoky haze lies over much of the area. The haze does not smell of smoke, but of sulphur and lava and decay. Boiling hot springs and lava lakes dot the surface. Some of the water pools are toxic – before traveling across this treacherous land you must know which to avoid, for if you drink the water from the wrong pool you will meet an untimely, excruciating death.

In the center of this hellish land is a wide and deep cauldron of bubbling lava. Even the sky looks like it's burning. Fiery clouds with spider holes hang low over the Cauldron.

Amazingly, the Gehenna people have adapted to this wasteland. They have been bred to withstand a land fit only for those with uncanny strength and very few needs. They are fierce, need little water, and can subsist on the insects and small mammals and rodents that scavenge here, and the few plants that cling to any damp patch of land. Their secret to survival is this adaptation to little food and water, their fierceness, and a healthy dose of determination.

The Land of Frozen Waters is an enchanting, mystical place. It is said that elves, ice fairies, and other magical creatures call this land of ice and snow their home.

The Northern Mountains lie to the north (fittingly); the Derryveagh Mountains to the east. And interestingly, the southern border of this icy wonderland is the hot and desolate Gehenna. Along this border of fire and ice is an amazing sight. Steep cliffs stand tall and strong, like soldiers at attention. Their craggy faces appear to have human features with hooded eyes, dour mouths that frown perpetually, and huge curly mops of hair formed from the leafy trees that grow atop them. These are the Cliffs of the Ancient Cromlech. Behind them, on the Gehenna side, a wide, impassable chasm that is believed to be the door to Hell and is appropriately called Hell's Door, stretches from the Derryveagh Mountains all the way to the Misty Mountains that border Fingal's Land.

In the Land of Frozen Waters lies a magnificent frozen lake that is so transparent it looks like glass. Uneven patterns, formed by ice that bubbles up into various types of ice sculptures, sit atop the surface in places, adding to the already magical landscape. If you were to take a walk through this artistic palette, you might believe yourself in a sculptor's workshop.

At the end of this massive lake are long cracks in the surface of the ice that make a surprising spider web effect. You might imagine these to be homes of monstrous woolly spiders, but you would be wrong. Nothing dangerous lives among these crevices – or anywhere else in the Land of Frozen Waters, for that matter. It is a glittering, pristine paradise where all creatures get along, though some are more likely to play pranks on unsuspecting travelers than others.

But who knows what anyone or anything is capable of when challenged?

Unbeknownst to anyone but Grayson, who knows more than he is likely to admit, and the elves, who are privy to some of his secrets, is the hidden tunnel that runs through the eastern-most edge of the Northern Mountains to the sea that surrounds all the lands of Grayson's domain. Inside the tunnel is a passage, hidden from view by steep stone walls on all sides. It is only wide and tall enough for a train to chug quietly through.

Only one has the power to summon the stunning arched bridge, built by elves at the beginning of time, that connects the tunnel passage to the secret train. But we will get to that.

Perched high upon the Northern Mountains, the Cosmic Caverns Tundra sweeps over the tops and sides of thousands of mountain acres, bleak and glacial, with a biting wind that is unending. It is barren and lonely, only the hardiest of creatures daring to venture there. It is, however, home to the sure-footed mountain goats, wooly sheep, hardy white hares, caribou, wolves, and a variety of birds. Salmon and trout inhabit its waters.

Vegetation grows low along the ground, providing the food needed for the animals to survive. The wolves are the only exception – these carnivores prey on the plant eating animals, and at times travel below the tundra, where the food is more abundant.

The Abbey That Time Forgot is south of the Gehenna and separated by a deep ravine and the towering mountains of the Omoud range. It sits in the Valley of the Forgotten Abbey and is unseen by any wanderer. Unless, of course, you are one of the chosen few who know where to look and the code that allows you to enter.

It is a gothic building of massive proportions, built by monks when this part of the world was an almost uninhabited place. It sits in a wide, bowl-shaped valley with steep, stony mountains surrounding it that are impossible for most creatures to scale. The two secret entrances were forged through the mountains to the south and west so that no part of the Abbey is visible. From the mountains themselves you enter the Abbey, which has a central courtyard where a profusion of flowers, herbs, vegetables, fruit trees. and nut trees grow.

You can see the spires from the courtyard or roof only. If you climb the steps inside the courtyard, you can reach the roof. From there the high mountains are visible and the vast sky can be seen to full advantage. The monks can access the rooftop and the mountains from several points inside the Abbey and walk among the mountain trees, visiting the great waterfall that plunges into a small river. The river's origin is a mystery. The monks of long ago followed the river to a small opening in the side of a mountain where it seemed to disappear altogether. But it provides them with all the water they need, and they are content with that.

Fingal's Land is a varied land of hills and fertile valleys. Small towns dot the area and are overseen and protected by Defenders. The villages are mostly self-sufficient and the people that abide there rarely venture far. The Defenders send scouts to communicate with nearby villages and to patrol the areas near their own village.

Hernsart, far to the north, is the largest town, followed by Bodun, which is located near the Abhanmohr River. But our story begins in the small village of Nil's Knob, close to the Fearann Draoidh, so let us begin.

THE DEFENDERS

Chapter One

There was once a gentle, wise man who lived high in the mountains above a meandering river. The Fearann Draoidh, or Wizard's Domain, towers at the curve where the Cagar and the Crystal Mountain ranges of Terrene meet. The vast woods continued the curve of the mountain to the northwest. The Great Southern Plains swept away to the northeast and Fingal's Land sprawled to the north. The Sea of Mists thundered at its back door.

Nestled in a curve not far from the river was a teeming village. Grayson watched over the peaceful village from his aerial perch. It was a thriving village – though that was about to change. Even now, the tides of change and destruction were headed toward the village. He bowed his head at the inevitable destruction and wished it would not come. He was not fond of war. Sighing, he continued to watch.

Down below, a woman came out of the hut closest to the river, straightening as she passed through the small opening. She frowned towards the river in the distance. She couldn't see it for the trees that blocked her view, but something seemed to pull her to it. With a shake of her head, she turned away and headed towards the creek that trickled along the edge of the village. Above her the sun blazed down and there were no clouds to bring reprieve from the incessant heat. Even so, a chill passed over her, prickling the skin on her arms, and causing a slight shudder to pass along her spine.

She walked down the wide path between the scattered huts. The owl was there, as she knew he would be, watching her from the wild plum tree. She paused to stare into his glittering yellow eyes before passing on below. His message was clear, and she quickened her step. She must get to Lucas and begin preparations.

The moment his name entered her thoughts, Lucas appeared beside her.

"He will not listen to our reports," he said, with clenched jaw and eyes stormy with anger. "I am no longer sure of him. He behaves like a fool! Or perhaps he has become too complacent?" He said this with remorse, for he had known McBride since childhood.

"We dare not wait," she began, but her gaze swung toward the distant thunder of hooves.

Lucas watched the lone rider crashing down the hill and ran to meet him. She began to tremble as she watched their exchange. After only a few words had been spoken, the man reached a hand to Lucas and swung him onto the horse's rump and galloped towards her.

In moments they were before her. Both men jumped to the ground, leaving the horse blowing and tossing his great head. Lucas grabbed her by the hand and headed toward their hut at a run. "It has begun," he spoke quietly. "They have over-run Trenton. That man is a Defender who was returning home. As he approached the village from the south, he saw the devastation and knew that he would be no help there. He has come to warn us."

Aggie ran into their hut, shaking the sleeping boy awake before grabbing the pack that stood always ready next to the doorway. The boy sensed her urgency and moved quickly alongside her, rubbing his eyes.

"Go quickly," Lucas whispered as he held them wrapped in his arms. Colin stared from one to the other with huge green eyes. His father smiled at him and held his son's upturned face in his massive hands for a moment, drinking in his features. Then he was gone.

Aggie tightened the pack on her back. "Remember the trail that we sometimes walk on to reach the caves high up over the river?" The boy nodded. "And remember the game we play on our way there?"

"The one where we don't talk and we race as fast as we can?" he asked, scrunching up his face.

"Yes. Today we must go even quicker and more quietly than ever before." She looked at him intently. "Do you understand?"

"Okay," the boy answered looking at her with serious eyes. "I get to lead, though."

Aggie smiled at his seriousness and silently thanked her husband for his wisdom. It was he who had sent them over and over again to the caves. He would save his son and his wife even if he must die, she thought grimly. He could not know that she had no intention of leaving him.

Colin took off at a fast clip toward the river. They were shielded from view on both sides now that they were in the trees, and the path, the size of an animal path, was easy to follow, though one must know its entrance before it was easily visible. They made little sound as their feet trod on the pine needle strewn path. The path was almost level, so they made good time.

The river was treacherous when the storms came and swelled the river waters, but today it flowed serenely towards the waterfall further downstream and into the deeper water where they kept their boats. None of the villagers knew of the path they walked, and Grayson had made sure they never would. Nonetheless, they were cautious when they ventured to the caverns. Colin moved off the path and led the way to the tiny, camouflaged bridge a quarter mile away through dense evergreens.

No words were allowed, so when they had crossed over, Colin looked back at Aggie to see if he was to continue in the lead. She smiled at him and motioned for him to go ahead. He obediently picked up his pace as he led the way up. They were climbing higher now into the fog that always hung there, and he began to pace his breathing as he'd been taught.

He looked back as they neared their usual resting place, but his mother motioned him on with an almost imperceptible flick of her wrist. He was happy to keep moving. His eyes flitted along the path, occasionally picking up signs of animal passage. He listened as a hawk screeched overhead. Further along a squirrel chattered until Colin got near and he abruptly quieted. The air smelled clean, and though no breeze touched him in the close confines, he could hear the rustle of the wind in the tall trees overhead.

As the trees began to thin, he looked for the path that skirted the hill. It led him through a narrow passage of stone and along a rocky ledge to the caves. He stood in silence as his mother approached and stopped beside him. She motioned that she would lead, and he fell in behind her. He was puzzled at the route she took. He had been into only one of the caves, but she headed away from that one.

He followed in silence as she led him higher along the mountain. A thin mist continued to swirl around them. He could hear running water, but saw nothing. When it looked like they were approaching a dead end, he hesitated, but his mother continued sure-footedly forward and disappeared from view. He hurried towards what he thought was a wall and saw his mother reappear from behind it. He realized that anyone following the path would continue curving to the left, but there was a hidden entrance in the wall to the right that led to a short tunnel. When they neared the end of the tunnel, Colin was amazed to see a well-kept garden with a small stream running through it, and a man walking towards them.

"I've been waiting for you," the man said as he hugged Aggie to him. "And this must be Colin." He reached out to shake his hand. The boy was getting tall, almost reaching his shoulder. "Come," he said gravely. He led them through the garden to a table made from a great gray boulder. On it were cheese and bread, as well as some cool water in a pitcher. He handed them each a cup of water and motioned towards the food.

"Colin," Aggie said, "this is Grayson. He and I must talk. Why don't you eat some of the cheese and bread?"

Colin was ravenous and took what he was offered. He sat on a rock and looked around him with interest.

Grayson led Aggie to a stone bench far enough away that they would not be overhead by the boy, but close enough that they could keep an eye on him.

"It has begun," Grayson remarked without preamble, his gray eyes penetrating hers.

"Yes," she answered. "A Defender who was returning home to Trenton saw his village destroyed. He rode to warn us, and Lucas is trying to rally our village. McBride has not listened to our warnings, but perhaps he will listen to someone who has seen the destruction firsthand."

"I fear he will not," was the reply. "He has grown too complacent these years and feels his power too strongly. He has sealed his own destiny. But what of the people?"

"There are few Defenders in the village, and I don't believe the villagers will rally in time to offer much assistance in its defense."

"What will the Defenders do?" He watched her carefully.

"We will fight, of course." she said defiantly. "What else can we do?" She looked at Colin innocently wandering around the garden, and her eyes misted.

"You said 'we', but did not Lucas send you to me for protection?"

"Lucas believes I will stay because he ordered it so," she said wryly.

Grayson studied her face and sighed at the determination he saw written upon it. "But you won't be staying, I gather."

"I am a Defender, same as he, and I will not hide in the caves while he and others fight." She looked at him sadly and drew a long breath. "You must take care of Colin. We will return for him if possible."

He glanced over at the boy, and then down at his hands before turning to face her. "There is another way."

She looked sharply at him.

"You must gather the villagers that will listen to you, as well as the Defender from Trenton. Take the boats and sail quickly to Alfred's village. You will find refuge there."

Aggie jumped up and opened her mouth to protest but sank back onto the bench when he raised his hand for her to not interrupt until he had finished.

"You will have time to gather supplies there and you can join forces with other Defenders from across the land." He stood and walked over to a low portion of the stone boulders that formed a natural wall and looked down at the valley below. "That is the only way."

"Run?" she whispered incredulously. "Is that what you're suggesting? We are Defenders. Our duty is to those who look to us to save them. We are not cowards who skulk away in the night!" She held herself erect and stared at his back.

Grayson turned and looked at her piercingly. "Then you will all die. You know this to be true. You are outnumbered ten times. Nay, one hundred times. If the Defenders die, or worse, become captives, what have you gained? The entire country will lie in ruin. Because of what? Pride?" He spat the word out.

He continued to stare at her, his countenance grave and his eyes flashing. "Go. Tell Lucas what I have said."

Her gaze fell before his and she turned away. Colin was sitting on the ground, lost in a boy's world of insects, colored stones, sticks, and other materials he had gathered around him. He was holding a huge black beetle captive in a tiny stone fort, marveling at his new pet.

Aggie blew out a breath and went over to squat on the ground beside him. His smile warmed her as nothing else could; yet broke her heart as she recognized the probability of never seeing her son again.

"I must go, Colin," she said quietly. "Papa and I will come for you as soon as we can." She blinked the tears away and wondered if she should give him that hope. But without hope, how could she or he survive? She swept him into a big hug. "You will be staying here with Grayson for a while." She held him away from her and smiled. "There's so much to explore here, the time will pass fast, and your father and I will be back before you know it." Now she was outright lying, and she knew it, but was it so wrong?

"Will you be back tomorrow?" he asked, wrinkling his forehead and frowning.

She smiled and shook her head. "No, it will be longer than that. Grayson will take good care of you. You are growing up so quickly and have much to learn from him, so heed his directions well. He is a great teacher, and this is a wonderful place to learn. You will have more fun than you can imagine."

She kissed his cheek and stood, removing the cross that she always wore and placing it around his neck. "Your Papa and I love you more than anything in the world and will come for you when we can." After hugging him tightly, she turned to go as Grayson came to stand beside Colin, his hand on the boy's shoulder.

"God speed, Aggie," Grayson said softly. And then she was gone, racing down the mountainside to stand beside her husband and the other Defenders to face whatever fate awaited them.

Chapter Two

It was chaos down below. Aggie raced at a rapid but even pace towards it, her mind a blur of jumbled thoughts at first, until she quickly ordered them into a plan of action. In moments, it seemed, she was down the mountain and crossing to the meeting house of the Defenders. Grayson watched as she loped from the forest and into the open, before turning his attention to the boy, who stood silently next to him.

As Aggie entered the room, the man from Trenton was speaking. "There are at least a hundred men headed your way. Trenton was already ablaze when I arrived." His eyes were hard, and he spoke boldly. An effort, Aggie thought, because he surely had family that were now lost. "The marauders may not tarry there for long. We have, at most, until early tomorrow before they are here. They won't expect you to know about Trenton, but how long they wait will depend on what they find there." His voice trembled with emotion as he stared at the Defenders gathered before him. "You haven't much time."

Aggie's eyes swept over the crowd until she found Lucas, and as she hurried toward him, squeezing through the men and women in the room, a loud voice interrupted the meeting.

McBride strode through the room, scattering people as he shoved through. He was a massive man with a strong build, raven hair, and steely dark eyes. "We have plenty of time to prepare!" he shouted. "The marauders won't leave their pillaging until the last person is dead and the last building burned."

Aggie winced at his words. While true, she didn't like to think of those poor people, whole families and brave warriors, lying dead in a burned-out village. She was glad when Lucas interrupted him. "McBride, you need to leave! You are not a Defender and have no voice in what we decide." His penetrating eyes glittered dangerously at McBride. He had much more to say to the man who called himself the village leader, but now was not the time. "Now!" he said loudly.

Thirty-five sets of eyes stared at McBride. His face reddened, but he managed to hold his tongue, turned on his heel, and stomped outside.

Aggie's breath whooshed out. One catastrophe avoided. For now. She reached Lucas's side and quickly repeated what Grayson had suggested. Lucas looked at her blankly for a moment, then responded, puzzled. "He wants us to *run?*" he whispered skeptically.

She nodded and spoke quietly. "He may be right, Lucas. He always is. Though the thought of running is contrary to all we believe in."

As Lucas tried to digest the thought of fleeing, she spoke again, hesitantly. "Do you think it cowardly?" Lucas stared at her as she added, "Or smart?"

Lucas pulled his eyes from her and looked out over the crowd. Even if it saved everyone's lives, these people would never agree to run. They knew nothing about Grayson, the Dragon Master, nor could he tell them. He would have to convince them himself or the entire village would soon be lost. For he agreed with Grayson. If they could reach Bodun, Alfred's village, they would have a chance.

As his thoughts whipped like wind through his brain, a plan began to form. "Listen to me for a moment." He held up his hand for quiet and the rumble of voices stopped. "The marauders will be upon us too soon for us to mount an adequate defense. Whether it's a few hours or a day, we haven't enough time. We are brave people and seasoned fighters, but we are not foolish." He searched the faces of the crowd. They were listening.

"Most of us have families, and you all know that no matter how well we fight, we cannot fight one hundred seasoned warriors and come out victorious."

His eyes moved from person to person, and he saw the first signs of doubt cross their faces. "Some of us were planning to head to Hernsart in two weeks, with stops along the way in other villages. Each of these villages has roughly the same number of Defenders as we do, some more. Preparations are already well under way." Some were nodding now, and he pushed his point. "If we take all the boats, there will be room for everyone in the village to depart. We just need to empty the storerooms and add more supplies, and we could leave in a matter of hours. We can warn the other villages along the way and build our forces into a large enough number to fight the marauders, if it comes to that, and win."

Confusion was written on the faces of some of the people gathered around him, but most seemed to understand what he was saying. He stepped up on a bench, so he could be seen by everyone. "We are too few to save this village. We will meet the same fate as Trenton and leave the path open for destruction of all the villages along the way to Hernsart. Each of us will die, as will our wives and husbands, children, mothers, fathers, brothers, sisters, and friends. Some may be taken prisoner, but we all know that is a fate worse than death."

Before anyone could speak, a short, wiry man pushed his way to Lucas and climbed onto the bench beside him. Lucas recognized him as one of the scouts from a village many miles away.

"The marauders are on the move. There are two villages in this area. One of them is mine and the other is yours. If we stay, they will destroy both villages. You may be the first or the second. We are almost the same distance from Trenton, but from what I can tell, they are headed here. I will advise my village to leave and my advice to you is to leave, also. We can join forces in Hernsart."

As soon as he uttered these few words, he stepped down from the bench and retreated the way he had come, looking into Aggie's eyes and muttering, "*Run*!" Before she could react, he was gone, his horse clattering away at a gallop.

The rumble in the room was growing louder. Lucas shouted to be heard. "We are running out of time. We must be in complete agreement. I say we leave. "What say you, Aggie?"

"I agree," she answered.

"Ishmael?"

"I agree."

Lucas took solitary votes from the ten people in the room he knew would stand with him. Their choice was to run and live, or stay and die. As the last of the ten agreed to leave, a battle- scarred hero of the grueling wars from many years earlier, shouted at the Defenders who were left. "We cannot fight this day! There will be another day to fight! To the boats!"

The crowd surged out into a darkening day. Many, those who inhabited the world of gentle manners, the subtle art of persuasion, and those who had nothing to fear, would've said their exit amounted to chaos. But looks can be deceiving. Each of these Defenders was a cog in a very well-oiled machine. Their training was ingrained, and while it had nothing to do with flight, because flight had never entered their minds before this day, they knew their parts in any travel plan, emergency or not, and hurried to make sure that their personal cog was in place.

Lucas breathed in deeply. Taking Aggie by the arm, he said, "Get Colin and meet me at the boats."

Nodding, she raced toward the mountain. As she neared the river, the owl flew toward her, his bright golden eyes boring into hers. He flew directly in front of her, making her stumble. He circled her, his great wings almost touching her, three times. She looked around wildly. They were out of time. The marauders must be closer than they thought. The owl was a messenger from Grayson.

As soon as that thought hit her brain, the owl turned and headed back to Grayson's Mountain, Fearann Draoidh. She would never make it up the mountain and back to the boats in time. Was that Lucas's plan? That she be returned safely to the mountain and Colin?

With a frustrated cry, she flung herself back down the trail. Colin would be safe on the mountain with Grayson. He wasn't expecting her back so soon, anyway. She knew that, but it didn't make her decision any easier. Her place was with the Defenders. She had taken an oath, and she would honor it.

As she entered the village, she was relieved to see the villagers with their animals, packs, and children headed on a trot toward the boats moored a half mile away in the thickest depths of the forest where the river flowed deep and clear. Her eyes flew from person to person as she urged them to hurry. She searched for Lucas as she ran.

She found him astride his big bay stallion shouting at McBride. "Go, or stay, I don't care. The boats are leaving within the hour. If you aren't on one, you will be left." He was holding the reins of her fidgety mare and Colin's pony. Apparently, he *had* expected her – and Colin - to return.

"We're out of time," she said, as she took the reins from him and swung onto the back of Dahlen Ghea. He looked askance at her. "Colin?"

She shook her head, "Not enough time." He stared at her but didn't question her statement, for she knew things he did not. Leaving McBride standing, mouth agape, they galloped toward the fleeing villagers, who were now out of sight in the forest. They didn't look back. Neither was interested in what McBride and his few followers did.

Lucas had toyed with the idea of burning the village but had decided against it. McBride and his men might decide to stay and would need shelter, though shelter wouldn't mean much to them if the marauders came and killed them. But a village ablaze would be visible for miles, warning the marauders that something was afoot. There was very little left, anyway. They were taking everything but the structures with them to Bodun.

As they loaded the last of the villagers, their supplies, and animals, onto the boats, Lucas didn't know whether to breathe a sigh of relief or frown in dismay as he saw McBride and his men slink aboard the boat behind his. Their eyes met briefly before McBride looked away.

As the boats reached the middle of the river, Aggie was lost in thought. Lucas came and put his arm around her, and they stood silently until Lucas kissed her on her forehead and smiled into her tear stained face. "Colin was expecting to stay, and even though he will miss us, and we will certainly miss him, he is safe and that's all that matters."

Aggie sighed. "I know, but it still seems unreal." She swiped her cheeks and eyes and faced the direction where the hidden mountain lay. Neither she, nor anyone, could see it, but she knew where it was and watched it until the curve in the river swept the boats away.

Lucas turned them both to face forward and looked out over the water. "Let's hope that the war will be over soon."

Aggie leaned against him and breathed in the clean, fresh air. She smiled at the thought of the adventures awaiting her son. She wouldn't mourn. He would've gone to Grayson sooner or later; it was just a bit earlier than she had intended.

Chapter Three

High on the mountain, Grayson watched them leave and nodded. They had taken his advice. Good. The marauders could not be stopped by one village, no matter how bravely they fought. Perhaps the Defenders would make a stand once they had gathered in unity. He didn't doubt that it would happen, but he shivered nonetheless, pulling his cloak more closely around him. It was all he could do not to interfere in the workings of men, but their fate was not his to decide. Giving advice to Aggie was the one thing that he could do - for now. He must be an observer, but he would watch closely. Terrene deserved to survive, and if it came to it, fate or not, he would throw all his power into the fray and fight alongside its quite varied inhabitants.

Turning away from the ledge, he saw that Colin was back at the table and was intent on building some type of structure with the rocks he had gathered from beneath the ledge. The ledge was tall and strong and hid the caverns from sight, but small rocks fell from time to time, which he usually replaced. They would do just as well as building blocks for Colin for now.

The mountain was indistinguishable to ordinary people. There was no way up unless one knew exactly where to look and how to unlock the way. The ledges that hid the cavern entrances blended so well with the rocky outcroppings, no one would guess that someone lived behind them. And when it mattered, the mountain was cloaked in a cloudlike fog that acted as an impenetrable shield that most beings could not see through. No one came here but the few that Grayson trusted completely.

He filled a cup with water from the trickling waterfall near the vegetable garden. After drinking it greedily, he re-filled the cup and went to lean with his back against the wall, reaching to grab a bit of bread and cheese from the table as he passed.

Colin was engrossed in his own world and examined everything in his reach in the greatest detail. He was a curious boy. Grayson watched the beetle, still trapped in the enclosure Colin had caged him in. It was black, at least two inches long, with a curved horn on his head, strong mandibles, and ribbed grooves along his back. Before long he succeeded in loosening a rock from the pen and escaped through it. This drew Colin's attention and he and Grayson watched as the beetle scurried away, suddenly spreading his wings and with a disdainful look at the boy and the pen, flew into a tree just beyond the wall.

Colin rushed to the wall and examined the tree carefully but did not see the beetle. Grayson, however, did see him blending perfectly into the wood not far above the boy's head. His eyes twinkled as he saluted the beetle with two fingers. The beetle stared back at him for a moment before scuttling into the labyrinthine tunnels that ran throughout the tree.

Grayson pushed himself off the wall. There were only crumbs of bread and cheese left on the table and he knew that various creatures would make short work of them once he and Colin were out of sight.

Stepping beside Colin, he asked, "Do you know what kind of beetle that was?"

Colin shook his head and looked up at Grayson. "I've not seen one like him before."

"That's because they are only found here on this mountain."

The boy's eyes widened. "Only here – out of the whole world?"

Grayson smiled. "That's right. He is a Great Horned Warrior beetle."

Colin looked thoughtful for a moment. "I like that name. It serves him well."

Grayson nodded. The boy would learn one day just how well the name fit. But for now, "Come along, then," he said.

Colin followed him back into the tunnel that he and his mother had traveled through. Several feet inside the tunnel were narrow stairs that led up and up to his right. *Funny*, he thought, *I don't remember those being there.* He halted, looking questioningly at them, before following Grayson up.

When Grayson had climbed maybe twenty steps, the boy right behind him, he looked back over his shoulder and winked at Colin. Colin hesitated and then looked behind him, gasping as he saw that there were only three steps behind him, the rock wall solid behind them. Grayson chuckled silently and continued climbing.

Colin couldn't keep from glancing over his shoulder every few steps. He always found three steps and the rock wall, as if they were making no progress at all, *or* the steps they had climbed were disappearing! He shook his head. What kind of place *is* this?

As they neared the top of the steps, they faced another solid rock wall, but Grayson merely turned a short corner, walked around a large boulder, lay his hand on the side of the boulder, and the wall opened just enough for them to squeeze through before closing silently behind them.

They entered a small cavern with an eerie greenish glow. Colin noticed that green ferns grew on the sides. Huge half-pillars jutted up from the floor in places, and high above his head were sculpture-like formations. It was light inside the cavern and Colin could see the sky in places where the top of the cavern had fallen in. Mushrooms grew in profusion, every color, size, and type one could imagine. Water dripped, forming shallow pools.

Grayson led the way to a silvery pool beneath a waterfall. "Let's wash up," he said, as he knelt beside the pool. Colin watched him splash water on his face and scrub his hands with some of the sand from the bottom of the pool.

Colin followed suit, running his wet hands through his hair as he watched Grayson doing the same to his unruly coarse gray hair and beard.

He sat back on his heels surveying the room. Beside the pool, two massive tree trunks rose from the floor to the fern and moss-covered ceiling. As he looked closer, he could tell that the trees were carved from stone, but the effect was that of ancient giant tree trunks.

Next to the waterfall lay a stone-floored opening that looked like the huge open mouth of a sea monster, not that Colin had ever seen a sea monster, but he could certainly imagine what one might look like. The long, jagged teeth bared menacingly. Colin could barely take in one thing before he was met with another astonishing sight. He was riveted by this magical place.

Grayson shook the water from his hands and led the way deeper into the cave. Colin knew nothing of caves but wondered how it could be so light deep within the mountain. His senses told him that it should be as dark as a starless night, but apparently that's not how it worked, for dappled light lit their way without a hint of a lantern in sight.

The smaller room, with the silvery pool, led into a much larger room. Colin stopped to look around as Grayson went to tend the cook pot over a low fire at the far side of the room.

This must be where Grayson lived. Unlike the smaller room, this one was dry. Pale light danced on the walls and across the smooth surface of the floor. In here, lanterns *did* sit on various outcrops and cast their glow into the room.

The fire crackled. A gentle breeze stirred the air. Beautiful woven mats were cast about underneath plump cushions next to a smooth tree trunk table set against one wall.

In the dimmer area of the room, where the light didn't quite reach, were several bedrolls stacked neatly over a thick carpet. Crevices in the walls held books, candles, clothing, cooking utensils, and other needed items. Colin marveled at it all as he explored. "That clothing is yours," Grayson said over his shoulder, as he went to check on the stew that was simmering over the fire.

"Thanks," Colin said as he hovered nearby. It never crossed his mind to wonder why there were clothes that were his inside the cavern.

"Come and take the bread from the oven," Grayson called, "and we'll eat."

Grayson's firepit was built into the side of the cave wall. Colin would find out later that the reason the room wasn't smoky was because the smoke was swept upwards and out through a circular pipe into a small opening in the roof above. The smoke would never reach the outside of the cave because there was a series of chambers it would have to travel through, dissipating along the way. These openings also supplied light, so that oftentimes during a sunny day the lanterns would not have to be lit at all.

Grayson was a cautious man. He wanted no one to see or smell smoke, nor did he want anyone to be able to gain access to the caves. He knew what could happen if he let down his guard. The spell he had placed over the entire mountain should hold, but one couldn't be too careful.

After their meal of stew and a heavy, grainy brown bread, Grayson showed Colin how to locate the hidden stairs that led to a small rooftop area open to the stars. The moon was halfway on its journey to becoming full and was just beginning to rise through the thin clouds that hung overhead.

As Colin sat down beside Grayson, he was suddenly overcome by the events of the day. He stared at the moon and wondered where his mother and father might be. His mother had told him once that every creature in the world looked up at the same moon. And the same sun and stars. Now he fingered the small polished cross she had placed around his neck and felt some comfort that wherever they were, they were all sharing the same moon. He sent a silent wish for their safety. How long would it be before he saw them again, he wondered. He could picture them clearly tonight, but would their faces fade from his memory in time? A tear trickled from his eye, and he didn't bother to wipe it away.

Grayson spoke softly from the shadows. "You will miss them terribly, but we must work diligently to prepare for their return. You have much to learn."

Colin stilled. "*Will* they return?"

Grayson turned to look at the boy. "What do you feel in your heart?"

Colin drew a deep breath as a series of memories clicked through his mind. His mother laughing, her eyes alight. His father hoisting him to his shoulders. His smaller hands holding onto their larger ones as they walked along. His mother placing the cross around his neck. "Will you return tomorrow?" he'd asked. "No, it will be longer than that," she'd replied. Colin smiled. They would be back.

"They will return," he answered Grayson confidently.

Grayson nodded. The boy needed to believe. And Grayson would do everything in his power to see that the boy and his parents were reunited one day.

Clapping the boy on the shoulder, he said, "We must rest. The day is not long in coming."

The fire had turned to a bed of twinkling coals. Once the lanterns were snuffed, the interior of the room had darkened, but still shards of light crept into the rocky crevices and along the stone floor.

The sleeping area was in an alcove next to the fire. They quickly laid out their bedrolls. Colin looked in wonder at the plush sleeping pallets. He was used to rolling up in a fur covered hide, or simply sleeping on a pile of straw. Grayson's pallets were magnificent – two hides filled with a goodly amount of fragrant grasses and sewn together,

As Colin crawled atop the cozy bed, he sighed and was asleep within five breaths. He didn't feel the soft-as-down woven blanket Grayson gently covered him with. Nor did he see Grayson lay his hand on each wall of the alcove, murmuring a blessing as he moved. Nor did he hear Grayson whisper, "Olcan, come," as he lay down upon his longer, thicker bed.

Grayson closed his eyes to the night, opening them a slit only for a moment as he felt the rough tongue lick his hand. He looked for a moment into yellow eyes that gleamed down at him. The man laid his hand on the massive head. "Welcome, friend," he whispered before falling into a deep slumber.

Colin was surprised at how busy every day was. Breakfast came early and consisted of one grain or another, salted and boiled to a creamy texture. With sweetening and butter added, it was a palatable meal. Occasionally, Colin found Grayson busily cracking eggs into a pan and then stirring them over the fire until they were set. He would divide the tasty eggs between them, and they would devour every tasty morsel.

The other meals differed from day to day, but usually came in stew form of one kind or another. Seasonal crops were foraged from the garden and the nearby forest. Common nuts and fruits were abundant. There were other foods that Colin had never seen before. Round red fruits that Grayson called pomegranates. Tasty brown sticky fruits called figs. Orange potatoes that were soft and sweet when baked in the ashes of the fire. Cheese and milk were always available. And Grayson mixed huge batches of a variety of greens with flower blossoms from the garden as a part of some meals. Mushrooms grew in the caves, as did several types of edible greens. They also enjoyed fish, pork, or chicken two or three times a week.

Grayson taught Colin how to tend the garden - how to prepare the land, plant, tend, and gather. And how to cook. Cooking was Colin's least favorite thing to do because he could easily be distracted from his meal preparation by some small creature that would slither, hop, or crawl along the wall or floor. Or the patterns of the light would subtly change. Or a host of other intriguing things would demand his attention. So dinner, when not burned, might be dry and tasteless, underdone, or seasoned with a too heavy hand.

Grayson never complained, but crunched along with Colin, trying to keep his face passive and his teeth unbroken. He was determined for Colin to learn, so he would eat whatever Colin put in front of him – within reason. Sooner or later, if he persevered, he knew that Colin would learn to focus enough on what he was doing to be able to prepare appetizing meals.

Much time had passed when Colin began to wonder where all the food came from. It began to strike him as odd that he never saw an edible animal except the few fish that swam languidly in the cave pools. Where did the chicken, pork, milk, cheese, and butter come from?

He knew that cheese and butter came from milk, but he had never seen Grayson make either. Where did the milk even come from? No goats or cows roamed about that he knew of. And, though they occasionally had rabbit stew, he had never seen a rabbit, alive or dead, anywhere but in the stew pot.

Colin puzzled over this for several days, keeping his eyes and ears open trying to learn how Grayson obtained the ingredients for their meals. He knew that the baskets brimful of earthy bounty came from the garden and that the nuts and fruits were foraged from the forest. The mushrooms came from the cave, or the shady perimeters of the forest. But for the rest of it, he had not a clue.

One day, as Colin watched Grayson cooking three nice sized fish on stones in the fire pit, turning them to get them evenly browned, he thought this would be the opportune time to find out where they came from.

"Where did you catch the fish?" he asked, as nonchalantly as he could.

Grayson darted a look at him before turning back to his task. With his back turned, his lips curved upwards in what could almost have been a smile.

"Where do you think they came from?" he asked, as he deftly removed the fish to two wooden plates, handing one to Colin and motioning towards the table. A healthy serving of fresh greens, chunks of fragrant brown bread and cold water awaited them as they plunked their plates down and sank onto their cushions.

Colin waited for Grayson to say the same prayer he offered at every meal - "We are blessed by this bounty" – before tasting a bite of fish and chewing thoughtfully, thinking about Grayson's question. He shook his head. "I have no idea."

He pushed his hair away from his face and picked up another piece of the flaky, delicious fish. When he finished chewing, he ventured a guess. "You must catch them from the waterfall pool."

Grayson raised his eyebrows and chewed noncommittally.

"Or from the creek in the garden?" His forehead furrowed. "Or maybe there's another stream that flows through the cave – or even further afield in the forest?"

Grayson answered Colin's question with a question of his own. "How much of the day am I out of your sight?"

Colin grimaced. Grayson was rarely out of his sight and then only minutes at a time. But not to be outdone, he said, "Maybe you go fishing at night while I'm asleep." He stared at Grayson as he awaited his answer.

Grayson was non-plussed, however, and bit off a huge piece of the bread as he thought. "I could do that, I suppose . . ."

"Ha!" interrupted the boy.

". . . but I don't," Grayson smiled. "I need my sleep as much as the next fellow." He was happy to see that the boy was thinking and observing.

Colin stared at him with narrowed eyes, suspicious that he might not be telling the truth. But Grayson ignored him, intent on chewing his meal.

When Grayson had swallowed the last morsel, he bustled away from the table in search of the strong ale he drank every night. Colin wrinkled his nose at the thought of the smelly brew, but Grayson seemed quite fond of it. He drank only a cupful, sitting next to the fire in his saggy old chair, the cushions shredded and worn, with his long legs stretched out to the heat. Sometimes he read, but as often as not, he sat still, his gaze on the flames.

Colin finished his meal and removed their dishes as Grayson slumbered before the fire. He took them to the shallow pool. The plates were so clean it seemed a waste of time to wash them, but he dutifully dipped them in the water, scrubbed them lightly with sand, and piled them in a bowl-shaped stone to dry.

When Grayson roused, he noticed the boy was fast asleep. He moved silently from his chair and laid out both bedrolls. He whispered for Olcan to come as he led the still sleeping boy to his bed. For a moment, he watched the boy sleep. He was so young, his face untouched by life. That would change. He sighed.

Grayson was interrupted in his reverie by Olcan, appearing beside him. The beast looked at the boy and then at Grayson before padding quietly to Grayson's bed and sprawling down beside it. Grayson went to bank the fire and check that all was secure. He touched the stones within the sleeping alcove, then patted the great shaggy head as he lay down, wrapping his warm cloak around him.

Chapter Four

The view from the top of Fearann Draoidh changed from day to day, sometimes subtly, such that one barely noticed a difference. Other times, quite noticeably – when the wind whipped the tall trees into a frenzy, or the clouds seemed golden instead of white, or gray, or black. Some changes were stunning, breathtaking. Occasionally, they seemed almost sinister. Those that lived on the mountain could see the surrounding land clearly, but anyone below saw only fog or the bare, steep wall of the mountain.

Colin sat on his favorite perch most days, the one that jutted out like a ship's bow on the eastern end of the vast rocky ledge that Grayson called a promenade. Colin had never heard of a promenade, but apparently it was some part of a large ship. It had a smooth rock floor with large flat boulders that formed a parapet, enclosing the entire area. It had the look of something put in place by design, but Grayson had assured him it was a naturally occurring boundary that had existed for millions of years.

Colin had been dubious. "How do you know?" he had asked. After all, millions of years was a very long time.

Grayson had peered thoughtfully at him before turning his gaze to the looming dark mountains in the distance, across the plains below. "Believe me, I know," he had said, turning and walking away.

Colin thought his answer queer, but just shook his head. Perhaps he did know.

Colin's perch was a table-like extension of the parapet that allowed him views of the open plains between the Fearann Draiodh, or Grayson's Mountain as Colin called it, and the mysterious inky mountains that lay shrouded in mist further to the east.

Today, individual sunbeams shimmered across the plains and lit the giant treetops near Grayson's Mountain to the west with a light like candle glow. The sky was blue gray, veiled by thin, wispy clouds. A gentle breeze blew across his face, lifting the ends of his hair away from his head. He gazed at the vista in front of him. Though the breeze blew on the mountaintop, not so much as a grass stalk quivered below.

As he stared downward, he suddenly became aware of an enormous shadow moving slowly across the plains, like the shadow of a small cloud that passes overhead and brings coolness for a moment to the ground below.

He got up on his knees and scooted to the edge of his perch. How odd! He squinted at the shadow, then raised his eyes upwards. The clouds were too wispy to make a shadow of any kind, let alone such a huge, dark shadow. He watched as the shadow advanced. Was it a shadow, or something more menacing? It was heading straight to the mountain Colin was perched upon. He shuddered and tried to call out to Grayson, who was working at his gadget wall at the far end of the promenade, but no sound came out. He wanted to run but couldn't move. The shadow was almost upon him. He stilled, transfixed, and braced for whatever might befall him as he heard a sound like lapping water on a shore.

Suddenly the shadow disappeared. Colin blinked. Did it crash into the mountain? There had been no impact, but the shadow was definitely gone. He looked around. Grayson continued at his work at his gadget wall, twisting one dial and making sparks fly. It didn't deter him. He merely nodded and turned the dial the opposite direction. Only the quiet of an ordinary day surrounded them.

Colin turned back towards the plains below. A darker swath marred the land, appearing like a trampled animal path from his mountaintop perch. The swath seemed to lie along the shadow's route from somewhere in the direction of the Misty Mountains and ending at the bottom of Grayson's Mountain.

As he puzzled over this oddity, Grayson called to him. Colin took one last look over the parapet and rubbed his eyes. The dark swath was fading away, and as he watched, it disappeared completely.

Grayson was beside him. "Come along," he said, placing his hand on the boy's shoulder. "We've got a lot to do." Colin wanted to tell Grayson what he had seen but could not find the words.

As they approached the opening that led into Grayson's sanctum, Colin searched intently for any telltale signs of the gadget wall, but there was none. Another mystery in the growing number of mysteries. Grayson disappeared into the murky light and the opening began to close. Colin quickly slipped through. Openings that opened and closed mysteriously, stairs that disappeared, food that magically appeared, peculiar shadows that darkened the ground below, gadget walls that vanished into thin air. It was all perplexing to say the least.

He could hear Grayson's soft footsteps moving ahead of him and he hastened to catch up.

As the days passed into weeks, then months, Colin continued to marvel at his surroundings. He began to appreciate Grayson's complex nature and intellect. The man was tireless, not only in his own endeavors, but in his, at times, almost obsessive desire to pass on his abilities and knowledge to Colin. And Colin tried to absorb it all. When he confessed his misgivings about all the intricacies of living in the cavern to Grayson, the older man just humph-h-hed and said, "You will be able to learn it all in time."

Grayson taught him more advanced numbers than he was used to, set him to learning chemistry, and let him read any of the books on the stone shelves in the living area. He practiced his writing until Grayson pronounced it readable. They walked together into the lighter fringes of the woods. Grayson wouldn't let him enter the deep gloom of the forest, pointing out the boundary he should never cross. As they walked, Colin learned to identify the trees and other plants. He learned them quickly and rattled off their names easily, so that he was impressed with himself, if Grayson was not.

Colin most loved the mysteries of the night sky. He had always been aware of the twinkling orbs above and was somewhat familiar with the phases of the moon. His people depended on this knowledge for their plantings and for their travels, but he did not know why until Grayson taught him.

Grayson pointed out the brightest star, which he called the North Star. He was amazed to learn that if he could locate the North Star, it would allow him to figure out the other directions. Rather than just having bright lights flung over the dark sky with no apparent plan, Colin learned that there are significant stars that will guide you. As Grayson pointed out these constellations, he told stories about them and explained how they shift in the sky during different seasons. Ursa Minor, Ursa Major, Perseus, Lynx, Draco, Cepherus, Orion, and others became as familiar to Colin as the names of the trees and plants he had learned. Draco was his favorite. Grayson explained that the name, Draco, meant dragon, and this constellation, according to mythology, represented Ladon, the dragon that guarded the gardens of the Hesperides.

One moonless night as they lay on the stones of the cavern rooftop staring up at the stars, Colin remembered the shadow that flew over the plains between the Misty Mountains and Fearann Draiodh and asked Grayson about it. Grayson was quiet for so long Colin thought he must have nodded off, and squinted his eyes at him.

As he opened his mouth to repeat the question, Grayson sat up, bending his torso over with hands clasped out in front of him, stretching, before getting to his feet. He reached his hand down to pull Colin up, and said, "That sounds quite mystifying." Without another word he headed off the rooftop.

"So, what do you think it was?" Colin asked as he hurried to catch up. He wasn't going to take a non-answer to his question, even from Grayson.

Grayson shrugged. "Why don't you show me the path that it made tomorrow morning?"

Colin's shoulders slumped. He knew there was no visible path left to see. "Well," he began uncertainly, "the path is no longer there."

"Well, then," Grayson mumbled as he lit his pipe and folded his long form into his chair, splaying his legs out in front of him. "Perhaps it will come again."

There was no more talk of odd shadows, but it didn't keep Colin from wondering about it.

One bright, warm day, as Colin toiled in the garden making a fence for the beans to climb upon, Grayson appeared and presented him with a staff similar to his own, though smaller. It was made from a small hickory trunk that had been peeled and smoothed. It was longer than Colin's height, but shorter and more lightweight than Grayson's. And unlike Grayson's, Colin's staff had short roots intact at the top with three small sparkling glass orbs inlaid among them – one purple, one blue, and one iridescent. It was strongly made, even the short roots jutting out from the top were thick and solid.

As Colin gazed at the staff in wonder, not daring to believe it was truly his, Grayson touched the staff below the roots and Colin started when the roots tightened around the orbs, completely concealing them.

Before handing over the magnificent staff to Colin, Grayson announced, "Every boy needs a staff of his own. Especially here on the mountain. You will find it to be very handy indeed."

Looking intently at Colin, he said firmly in a voice that brooked no argument, "You will not need the mechanisms at the top for now. You must learn your staff's purposes and strengths a little at a time. Until you advance in knowledge and power, you must promise me that you will not experiment at all, in any way, on your own."

Colin grinned up at Grayson. Was he teasing him? Like some stick might be dangerous or something! Sure, he was pleased to have one of his own, but Grayson never did anything with his own staff but carry it around with him anytime he left the cavern.

His grin faded as Grayson's eyes glimmered and his scowl darkened.

"I . . . I promise," he stammered.

"*What* do you promise?" Grayson demanded.

Colin stood taller and looked into Grayson's scowling face. "I promise I won't experiment with my staff on my own."

With a final piercing look, Grayson relented. "A man is judged by his honor. I will hold you to that promise."

He handed Colin the staff. "Now let's get started," he announced as he led the way to the nearby meadow.

Colin was limp with fatigue by the time Grayson announced, "That's enough for today." He looked at Colin and hid a smile. The boy looked like he'd walked ten miles in a windstorm. His hair was a wild tangle, and his clothes were in disarray, twisted, and less than tidy. He had dirt smudges on his face and clothes where he had fallen several times as they had thrust and parried across the open expanse of the garden meadow. A staff was used for many things, defense included. Colin now had a tiny taste of the power of owning a staff.

Grayson bowed to Colin, who quickly returned a nod of his head and stood with his staff by his side as he had been taught to do. "Let us put our staffs away and then perhaps you might like to bathe in the pool and change into something a bit cleaner before you finish the fence. I will be out to join you shortly."

They placed their staffs side by side in a corner of the sleeping room. Colin watched through sweaty eyes as Grayson strode away, erect and with a purpose, his hair still neatly pulled back and fastened at his neck, his clothes spotless, his body clean and dry.

Colin wiped his eyes with his grimy hands, pushed his hair out of his face causing it to stand on end even worse, and looked down at his own soiled clothing. He straightened his tunic and jerked his pants around with a huff before plodding barefoot to the pool.

The days passed in this way, with the man and the boy gardening and harvesting, storing the fruit of their labors, foraging for more. They read and discussed what Colin had learned. Colin learned to calculate numbers in every way imaginable and continued to impress Grayson with his keen mind. He learned to cook, not nearly as well as Grayson, but one grew tired of burned, ruined, tasteless food. It was a matter of survival he came to believe. Boy and man practiced with their staffs, and Colin became adept at blocking Grayson's blows – and even landing one occasionally, though he was never sure whether Grayson only allowed him to land the occasional jab, or if he had actually done it on his own. He was pretty sure it was the former.

Colin grew familiar with the daily changes wrought by nature and could predict rain and storms by the sky and the clouds. He watched the fog over the eastern range of the Misty Mountains grow dense and ominous, shrouding the mountains from sight more often. The haze over the Mistys was different, more threatening, he thought, than the mist that veiled Fearann Draoidh.

At times he felt, more than heard, a slight thrumming in the air. Grayson pretended not to notice it, but Colin saw his eyes drift towards the mountains and his brow pucker. He even found him once on the high ledge where they observed the sky at night, with an instrument to his eye aimed towards the fog shrouded mountains.

When Grayson offered Colin a look through the telescope Colin didn't notice Grayson surreptitiously changing the focus so that Colin could not see through the fog as he had. Colin never knew how closely Grayson watched the crystal embedded in his staff. It had begun to grow murky, a worrisome development.

One day Colin called to him from his ledge and pointed towards the mountains. The fog had lifted and the sun shone down on the mountains, casting them in a more natural light. Colin had not noticed any thrumming for two days.

Grayson nodded and walked over to peer at the mountains, only the slightest mist hovering over the cliffs. He clapped Colin on the shoulder, searched the mountains for a few minutes, nodded his head again, and returned to tinkering with his gadget wall. Perhaps this lull would last.

Chapter Five

It had taken several grueling weeks to reach the village of Bodun. For Aggie, it seemed like a lifetime ago that she had said goodbye to Colin on Grayson's Mountain.

She and her fellow villagers from Nil's Knob had suffered much after what seemed like a narrow, but propitious escape from the marauders that threatened them. On the journey they had lost two villagers to unfortunate accidents. They had lost two more when a young woman and her unborn infant succumbed to the rigors of the journey.

The marauders had not reached any of the villages they had passed on their journey from Nil's Knob, which had surprised Aggie, while also giving her hope. Along Fingal's River during their weeks of travel, they had encountered several villages set on high slopes not far from the banks of the river. Several Nil's Knob representatives, including Lucas, had visited the villages to barter for supplies and to warn them of a possible attack from marauders coming from the east. The village leaders had heard them out but had had little concern that they were in any danger. "Our scouts have reported no activity, and even if they do, we will stay and protect our land," was the gist of their response.

The village leader of Fir Bolg professed that his village was protected by the melogs, strange creatures that were said to reside in the river and keep it from harm. It was frustrating, but when the Nil's Knob villagers had to leave their boats in the care of that very village as they traveled overland to Bodun, some hoped that the village leader was correct and perhaps the melogs would protect their boats.

McBride and his four followers decided to remain at Fir Bolg. "The marauders have surely retreated back across the border by now," he announced. "They will not bother us here." Could he possibly be right? The marauders seemed to be inactive now, but the lands of Terrene were vast and who knew if they had attacked outlying villages that they did not know about?

Even Aggie and Lucas had moments when they questioned their hasty decision to follow Grayson's suggestion and leave Nil's Knob. But as Aggie repeated often to herself and to Lucas: Grayson wouldn't have advised them to run if he doubted the wisdom of leaving. He wouldn't have insisted they do something so life-altering as to uproot a whole community if he wasn't convinced that it was the only choice they had if they were to save not only their own lives, but perhaps all of Terrene in the bargain.

So, during their last weeks before reaching Alfred's village, they continued to warn villages they passed about a possible attack and urged them to take precautions.

And tonight, as they straggled into Bodun, Alfred's village, the owl was sitting atop the watchtower at the entrance gate. As Lucas requested entrance into the walled town, Aggie felt, rather than saw, the owl. Glancing up, her eyes locked onto the grave, yellow eyes of the owl. She quickly looked away to keep from drawing attention to the creature that was Grayson's messenger to her. He would find her again when she was alone.

The weary travelers were welcomed to Bodun with open arms. Alfred was shocked to see them as he made his way through the crowd, but greeted them warmly. "*You* are the ragtag group of people that my scouts have reported heading this way?" He threw back his head and laughed, the scar across his cheek quite visible. The two men embraced. As they drew apart, Alfred announced to his people, "This is Lucas. I grew up with him." He smiled. "Too many years ago. Right, brother?"

Lucas grinned back at him. They were not blood brothers but were raised together and were as devoted to each other as the closest of brothers. They had not seen each other in over twelve years – since Lucas and Aggie had become husband and wife and settled in Nil's Knob. Alfred did not know they had a son, and for now, Lucas would keep it that way.

"And this," Alfred continued, grabbing Aggie's hand and pulling her forward, "is his beautiful wife, Aggie." Aggie blushed as he swept her into a hug to the delight of both sets of villagers.

The Bodun villagers all began talking at once, welcoming the strangers and accepting them into their midst solely because they had ties to Alfred, a leader who was as well-liked by them as they were by him. It was a content town. They had rarely known hardship and attributed much of their good fortune to their smart, strong leader. This did not mean they were soft, however. Their Defenders were among the strongest and most reliable of the entire country, having been tested in a long ago, hard-fought war that they could never forget. All of Bodun's villagers were fierce in their loyalty to Alfred and their land.

Alfred held up his hand to quieten the throng gathered around him. Pointing towards two men in the crowd, he said, "Matthew, John, please take our guests to the church grounds and ask Father Michael to make them welcome. They will be tired from their long journey."

As the two men strode forward, Alfred spoke to the Nil's Knob villagers. "Tonight, we celebrate! Go and make yourselves comfortable. Father Michael will show you where to camp and will make sure you have water and a place for your belongings."

Noticing that many of the travelers led horses, he added, "Matthew, please ask Ben to house the animals." Looking at Lucas, he asked, "Are there other animals that need tending?"

Lucas shook his head. "The herdsmen have remained outside the walls with the other animals. If, perhaps, you could send some food to them, they will be fine for the night."

Alfred smiled reassuringly before turning his attention back to the throng of guests and asking them to join him at the celebration in the town center next to the church as soon as the bonfires had been lit.

When the visitors were well on their way, followed by many of Bodun's citizens, Alfred's smile disappeared. "Come," he said, briskly walking away. Lucas and Aggie followed, leading their horses, wanting to keep them near.

They left the horses with Alfred's stableman and were soon ensconced in his modest home with refreshments in front of them. Alfred asked his housekeeper, Maisie, to help settle their other guests at the church.

"Take whatever you have in the way of nourishment. Father Michael might need your help for a while if you don't mind the interruption to your day?" She nodded and turned to go. "Oh, and there will be a celebration at dusk in the square next to the church to welcome our friends to our town. Will you help with refreshments for that, also?"

Maisie rolled her eyes at Alfred in a most un-housekeeperly fashion, leaving wide grins on Lucas's and Aggie's faces as she flounced from the room.

Alfred shrugged, meeting his friends' eyes with a sheepish grin.

They made small talk, sampling Maisie's delicious honey cakes, coarse brown bread and butter, cheese, and pear slices, until she had left the house. Then Alfred didn't waste time with further pleasantries. "What is going on?" he asked.

Lucas and Aggie exchanged looks - it didn't take Alfred long to move on to the heart of the matter. Aggie chuckled at the quick change in his demeanor. "So, you think it odd for our entire village to embark on a long, exhausting journey just to visit you?"

It was time for Alfred to roll his own eyes. "I think it highly unlikely that this is just a social call."

Lucas snorted. "And you'd be right. As usual," he ribbed Alfred. "But, moving on to the crux of the situation," and he began to explain what had brought them there, Aggie interjecting at times. Alfred did not interrupt until they had completed their story, except to ask a couple of probing questions about their actual journey and the villages they had stopped in on their way to his door.

He sat with hands clasped under his chin listening attentively.

"We are not sure if the marauders destroyed any other villages except the one, or even if our village was destroyed," Lucas finished.

Alfred continued sitting, looking intently, first at Aggie, then at Lucas, before turning his gaze to the wall in front of him.

He had been so still and quiet that he startled Aggie and Lucas when he suddenly stood and began to pace. "What made you go?" he suddenly asked. His shrewd eyes swept over them as they sat silently. They had intentionally not mentioned Grayson's part in their decision.

Running a hand over his short hair, Alfred dropped back into his chair and let out a long breath when they didn't immediately answer. "Grayson." The name that Lucas and Aggie had never said aloud to anyone but each other - and recently to Colin - was spoken almost casually by Alfred.

"Don't look so surprised. It's true that few people know him and that's as it should be, but I happen to be one of them." Waving a hand at Lucas and Aggie, he said thoughtfully, "You apparently are two more. And Hagan of Hernsart is another."

Thoughtfully rubbing his chin, he muttered, "This puts things in a totally different light."

Aggie looked puzzled. "What things?"

"Everything."

Aggie knew better than to try and hurry him along. She caught Lucas's eye for a moment before turning her attention back to Alfred.

"It is rumored, and verified by my scouts, and Hagan's to an extent, that a faction from the Gehenna lands, marauders as you say, are on the move. Nil's Knob is so far away from here, on the other side of the river, and most importantly, the closest village to Fearann Draoidh, that we never thought you were in any real danger. There have been unusual rumblings and darkness coming from the Gehenna lands. Our scouts have ridden as far abroad as the northern tip of the Gehenna that borders Fingal's Land, and to the northeastern part of the Southern Plains. Two of them have not returned, but those that have report a strange odor in the air and the look of a vast storm brewing. They also found a village in Fingal's Land, *our* land, that was completely razed." He paused to let that sink in.

"The scouts were very shaken and would not return to the borderlands. They have been keeping closer to home. We have an outpost near where the Abhanmohr flows from the Blue Forest. It is walled and heavily guarded. We are moving supplies into it as they become available. Hagan has set up an outpost in the Cosmic Caverns of the Northern Mountains. Some of our ships are moored on the Abhanmhor close to our outpost. Hagan's ships are readied and anchored on the Abhanmohr close to the border of The Land of Frozen Waters. We have only our fishing boats here and they will remain for now.

"So what are you saying, Alfred?" Aggie asked incredulously. "That war is imminent?"

A low knock sounded on the door and as they all three rose, Alfred held up his hand, motioning for them to stay as he went to open the door. That was okay with them as they could see and hear anyone who was at the door anyway, since it was just across the room. As Alfred opened the door, a small, bearded man greeted him. Without any preliminaries, the man announced in clipped tones that the village of Dunworth had been destroyed. "Just like the other one. Nothing is left but a horrible acrid smell and ashes."

Alfred quickly ushered him in and closed the door. He made no introductions but spoke quietly to the man. "Go to the church. Find Maisie and get supplies for your journey. Spencer and Red will be there. They can exchange your horse for another and then all of you ride out to all the villages within a two days' ride from here. The one of you that heads north go on to alert Hagan at Hernsart what has happened. Tell the village leaders to gather their villagers and supplies and head here if they are closer to us, or to Hernsart if it is closer to them. It will take time for them to prepare, but they must leave as soon as possible. Tell them that we fear an all-out attack and we must unite to defend Fingal's Land."

Alfred placed his hand on the shoulder of the man and walked him to the door. "Watch yourselves." The man nodded.

"We will alert our Defenders," Lucas said as the door closed. "But what of the other villages farther across the river?"

Alfred shook his head. "I fear we have no time and not enough riders to warn them." He rubbed a hand over his face. "You have already warned the villages south, along the river, but perhaps with this new news, I can send a boat downriver to warn them that there is no more time to dilly-dally. Perhaps they can send scouts to other villages, and so on."

He rubbed his hand over his troubled face. "We must have better information from the Gehenna area. It's hard to imagine that the Gehenna people, fierce as they are, would want war with us." He shook his head. "It makes no sense."

Aggie looked meaningfully at Lucas, who nodded slightly. "Lucas and I will scout the area near the Gehenna. We need to know exactly what to expect."

Alfred nodded, his face weary. "Yes, I thought you might. And, yes, we do," he said with a wry smile.

"But, tonight we celebrate as promised. It will give us a chance to have all our people together so we can break the news to them. In the meantime, talk to your Defenders and I will talk to mine. Quietly. Tomorrow at dawn, bring your best, most trusted five Defenders here and I will do the same."

As Aggie and Lucas started to leave, Alfred stopped them. "We will need to retrieve your boats from wherever you've left them. Since you will be gone soon, I presume, I will need you to assign some of your people to bring them upriver."

Chapter Six

The great gray owl came to Aggie that night long after the celebration had ended. She and Lucas had camped out near the others from Nil's Knob, falling into a deep sleep as soon as they had stretched out on their bedrolls. It was in the early hours of the morning that Quant flew soundlessly over her as she slept under the dark night sky. Though there was no sound, she awakened as quickly as if water had been poured over her and, easing herself away from Lucas's warm body, followed him some distance from the other sleeping villagers. The golden, glittering eyes were all that she could see in the total darkness as he dropped a gift from Grayson onto the ground at her feet before vanishing into the night. Aggie read the message that came with the gift. "Thank you," she whispered.

The next morning dawned clear and breezy. Aggie and Lucas spoke of the night's celebration as they headed to Alfred's, perhaps wanting to avoid thoughts of the difficult days ahead. The five Defenders they had chosen followed close behind.

Alfred met them at his door and ushered them into the same room they had visited in the day before. Five men stood as they entered. Alfred introduced them as Samuel, Joseph, James, William, and Ezra. They were all strong and capable fighters, though it had been some time since they were put to the test. An evil faction had crossed into Fingal's Land once before, but after days of onslaught, they were soundly defeated and vanquished. Since then, the people of Terrene had quietly gone about their lives. Not all of the Defenders were personally experienced in war, of course, but the ones who were not had been trained by the ones who were, and they all had survived other challenges and deprivations that had helped keep them strong as well.

The Nil's Knob Defenders were Ishmael, Marcus, Yiorgos, Liam, and Gerard. Only Gerard and Ishmael were old enough to remember the invasion, and they had never forgotten the horror and devastation. Both were still strong and fit but hoped they would never have to go through such times again.

Once the introductions were made, the men helped themselves to the breakfast set out on a narrow table against one wall. Alfred, Lucas, and Aggie took the chairs and the other men sat on the floor. As they ate, they discussed various plans at length before an agreement was reached. What Lucas and

Aggie would be doing was not discussed, but it was agreed that Alfred would take command of the villagers and the Defenders from both villages. His main tasks would be to oversee preparations in case it was decided that departure for the outpost, or for Hernsart, was imminent, to post more guards on the walls around the village and within the village itself, and to send some of the men to join those already at the outpost. Samuel, Joseph, and Liam were assigned to join the men at the outpost. They would report to the leader there, Murphy Byrne, and would carry a letter from Alfred that laid out their plans and any other information that was critical. Byrne was an astute man and would know what to do.

Gerard and Ishmael would take some of the villagers to retrieve the Nil's Knob boats from Fir Bolg and take them upriver close to the Abhanmohr. The rest - Ezra, William, James, Marcus, and Yiorgos - would remain in Bodun and help Alfred.

Red was already on his way to Hernsart to apprise Hagan of plans, including their plan to join him there if need be. He would also alert any villages along the way. Spencer was headed southeast across Fingal's Land, and Joshua, the wizened scout who had first alerted them to danger, was riding due east as far as he dared.

Back on Grayson's Mountain, the Fearann Draiodh, Colin sat in the sun dappled shade on his perch high above the Great Southern Plains. The frayed alchemy book that Grayson had assigned him to study had been set aside. Normally all the material about metals, their reactions, the curing of diseases, the four elements and how they worked, and other subjects within its pages excited him, but today he couldn't concentrate. He was daydreaming – the bane of all teachers.

Grayson startled him as he approached, though he was not trying to sneak up on him. Colin was just so far away in his own world, he jumped when he realized Grayson had called to him. His water cup went flying and if he had not already laid his book aside, it would most certainly have been damaged.

"What are you doing?" Grayson asked, though he had already taken in the abandoned book, and Colin's demeanor said all he needed to know about his lack of scholarly accomplishment. The boy hastily began to gather up his book, stuffing the papers inside, and picked up his cup, so Grayson bit back an admonishment and turned towards the door to the sanctum.

When Colin finally managed to slide off his perch and hurry after Grayson, he noticed that Grayson was already through the door. He watched in shock as the door began to slide into place. As he picked up his pace, he tripped and fell.

"Thunderation!" he exclaimed. He quickly gathered the papers that had flown from the book when it hit the stones, the book itself, and his cup and ran to the rock wall.

He hit the stone where the door should be with his hand. Solid rock. All he got for his effort was a shooting pain through his hand and arm. He stared at the solid rock wall, willing it to open. It didn't. He had never considered being locked out of the caverns before and had no idea what he was going to do.

"Calm down," he berated himself, breathing deeply. He laid his armful of materials aside and pushed his hair behind his ears. Grayson would soon discover that he was locked out and come and open the door. There was no sense screaming or banging. Grayson wouldn't hear him, and he had already experienced the result of human flesh against solid rock. He crossed his arms and watched the rock.

After quite some time, at least by his calculations, he concluded he was stuck. "Bother!" he exclaimed. Fidgeting, staring, hitting, and wishful thinking had not worked. He would have to come up with another plan. How did Grayson open and close the door? He tried to envision Grayson as he approached the door but could come up with no movement or action that he used. He pursed his lips and blew out a frustrated breath.

Suddenly he remembered Grayson laying his hand on a boulder to open another door. Maybe all the doors opened the same way. He looked around. The wall to the left of where the door should be was the gadget wall. When closed it became just another part of the seemingly impenetrable rock wall. His eyes fell on the large stone that jutted from the floor nearby. It was almost as tall as he was, and Grayson used it when he was working on the gadget wall to hold the small tools he worked with.

Colin approached the stone and examined it. Nothing remarkable about it. Feeling foolish, he reached out his hand and touched a place on the stone that might have been (to a very discerning eye) slightly depressed. He jerked his hand back as if he had been burned as the door slid silently open. Shaking the fog out of his head, he grabbed the materials he had laid aside and went quickly through the door. Once he was inside, the door closed noiselessly behind him.

As Colin entered the main cavern, Grayson looked up from setting their supper on the table. "What took you so long?" he asked nonchalantly.

Grayson appeared so unconcerned about Colin's absence, Colin burst out, "You locked me out!"

"Did I?" Grayson asked, motioning for Colin to sit down. "Let's eat. I nearly starved waiting on you."

Colin's eyes flashed as Grayson took his seat. When Colin didn't join him at the table, Grayson said, "Oh, that's right. You probably could do with a bit of a wash after your *hard* day at the alchemy charts." He flapped a dismissive hand at Colin, "Well, go on."

Colin clenched his hands at his side, drawing in a deep breath. "Aren't you at all concerned about me being locked out? I could've been . . ." He hesitated. Could've been what exactly? He realized that Grayson would not have allowed anything to befall him and would've come to check on him sooner or later. It was the "later" that concerned him. The whole incident was quite strange. Swallowing, he asked, "Don't you even want to know how I got in?"

Grayson smiled at him. "There's only the one way - for you - isn't there then? Go on now. Wash up."

Colin was quiet throughout supper and retreated from the room as soon as he had eaten. Grayson let him stew a while. If he had had any doubt at all about Colin's abilities, he had none now. He puffed out smoke from the pipe clenched between his teeth, the clenching quite necessary, else his grin would've allowed it to fall like lead onto the stone floor. He ordered his thoughts. It was time to seek out the boy. He hoisted himself up, knocked out his pipe and laid it aside, and went in search of his protégé.

He found Colin sitting on a stone beside the pool in the cavern, elbows on knees, chin propped on his folded hands. Grayson expected him to be upset, but when Colin looked up and saw him walking towards him, he grinned. "I opened that door just like you do!" he said smugly.

Grayson halted near the boy. "So you did, so you did," he agreed as he settled on a large stone next to him. Good, he thought, Colin's attitude might be a bit proud, but it was a wholesome, confident one.

"Let me see your hand." Grayson held out his own hand and took one of Colin's hands in his. Colin looked on, curious, as Grayson laid his hand palm up and stretched flat. Tapping on the smaller hand he held taut, Grayson spoke softly. "In your two hands is where the magic comes from. Your two hands hold power. You only need to learn to manage it safely."

Colin's eyes widened. Magic? Power? What was Grayson going on about? He watched Grayson doubtfully as his finger traced the lines in Colin's hand. "Each of your hands is different. *And* each line in your hand is not only different from your other hand, it is also different from everyone else's. Each tells you something about yourself." Grayson looked up from the hand he was examining to see if the boy was following him. Colin was staring at his hand as if it were some object he had never seen before.

Grayson smiled reassuringly and continued, lifting Colin's right hand up. "Your dominant hand is your right hand. It's the one you use most often. It shows you the direction your life has taken." Laying it back down, he tapped the left hand he was still holding. "This hand shows your character traits, a little about your personality, and certain aspects of what your destiny will be."

Colin stared at his hands, amazed, but also somewhat fearful of what Grayson was saying. He began to curl his fingers into his palm, but Grayson straightened them back out. "You don't have to understand it all today, but suffice it to say you are capable of considerable accomplishments. Do you understand?"

Colin continued to stare at his hands before raising his puzzled face to Grayson. "No."

Grayson shocked the boy by guffawing, unable to control his laughter until he finally noticed that Colin definitely did not see the humor in his one-word statement. Grayson's boisterous laughter then stopped abruptly. After clearing his throat for a full minute and then coughing, he managed to control himself enough to say, "Well, it's not that important for now. We'll talk more about it all later. In the meantime, you need to head to bed and try to get some rest. Tomorrow is a busy day."

As Grayson lay awake far into the night, the boy sound asleep, Olcan now keeping watch between them, he pondered how best to teach Colin what he needed to know in the most expeditious manner. The crystal in his staff and the one in the secret room upstairs were growing murkier, though for now he wasn't overly worried. Each time he looked at it he hoped to see the murkiness beginning to dissipate, but so far it held steady.

As he lay there unable to sleep, he clicked the wizardry training manual into his brain and began checking off each lesson. Some lessons he shuttled to the back of his brain. Others were imperative and must be dealt with quickly. Once he had a list firmly planted in his mind, he closed his eyes, emptied his mind, and slept. Only then did Olcan rest easy.

Chapter Seven

The next morning was blustery. A good day to stay inside. However, after breakfast and chores were completed, Colin went to get his staff as was the usual order of the day. As his hand touched the staff, however, he heard Grayson call, "Not today, Colin. We have other endeavors to attend to."

As Colin approached Grayson, he noticed yet another set of stairs had magically appeared in a wall that he had always considered solid. He shook his head. Would he never learn that very little was as it seemed on Grayson's Mountain?

They wound their way up and up and up in a spiral until they reached a solid wall in front of them. Sure enough, the stairs had disappeared, and they were standing in a short hallway with a huge, ornately designed door in front of them. Grayson did not touch a stone to enter this door but, instead, produced a large metal key and fitted it into the lock. With a click the door unlocked, and Grayson pulled the thick, heavy door open.

Colin's mouth fell open. He had never in his life imagined anything like the enormous room that stretched before him. He snapped his mouth shut when Grayson spoke. "You may look around while I get set up. That's *look*, not *touch*." He then strode over to one of the massive tables and began to sift through the items lying upon it.

The room curved at the far end, with windows that appeared to jut straight out into space like the prow of a ship. He walked towards them. The floor near the center in front of the windows contained a large pentacle. The circle was greenish blue and the five-pointed star within was purple. The colors glowed as if struck by sunlight. The five points of the pentagram touched the circle. A flat gray stone stood about three feet tall in the center of the pentacle and a bronze cauldron sat atop it, emitting a swirling mist of purples, silvers, golds, and greens into the air.

He tore his eyes away to look out the windows. The view was astounding. The fog that shrouded the Misty Mountains was dense and almost blue, completely wiping out the mountains and rolling in waves across the Great Southern Plains. Directly below him was Fingal's River, thread-like, and the Fingal lands. He could barely make out the tiny village of his birth, the buildings scattered about no larger than pebbles. He could distinguish no movement other than the fog; the river was too tiny for him to make out the current.

He moved away and began to walk through the room, not daring to touch anything, but absorbing it all. He had no idea what most of it was but was mesmerized, nonetheless. Sturdy tables squatted in no logical order around the periphery, stacked high with books, candles, incense, jars of every shape and size and color, crystals, and an assortment of implements. Tall shelves held even more books, and smaller shelves were filled with more bottles, rocks, sticks, and other paraphernalia. Overhead, magnificent crystals and yellow moons and stars levitated all around the room. An enormous copper-framed black obsidian stood to one side of the pentacle. It was at least six feet tall, and except for its shiny blackness, looked all the world like a mirror. He would later learn it was called a reflecting stone.

Ancient trunks hunkered beneath tables. Dragons made of carved wood encircled the rafters, their massive heads looking down toward the floor below. Next to the farthest bank of windows, Colin was startled to see a great gray owl fluffing his feathers atop a thick wooden perch. He stared at the owl, transfixed. He was silvery gray, quite large, with steady yellow eyes peering out of a round face; a most handsome creature.

"Meet Quant," Grayson surprised him when he spoke right next to him. The owl blinked languidly at Colin but showed no other sign of noticing him, twisting his head instead to stare reproachfully at Grayson.

"I know, I know. But it is time he is introduced to his calling," Grayson said to the owl. The owl looked unconvinced and flew up into the rafters to perch upon the back of one of the dragons.

Colin watched as the owl flew away, then turned to Grayson. "Did you really just talk to that owl?" he asked.

Grayson replied, "I did, indeed, just talk to Quant. He understands every language spoken. The trick is that you must understand *his* language." He raised an eyebrow at Colin before striding away. "Come along. We have work to do."

Colin held his tongue but was very skeptical of the idea of an owl understanding languages, let alone communicating. The owl never actually said anything after all, so how could he communicate? Colin shook his head and trudged after Grayson.

Grayson stood before a table with several objects strewn across it. He motioned for Colin to sit, and he then sat beside him. "There are benevolent wizards and malevolent wizards," he began without preamble. "Malevolent wizards practice magic for evil purposes; benevolent wizards seek to help."

He looked at Colin to be sure he had his complete attention. When he saw that Colin was listening attentively, he placed his hand over his heart and continued. "We are compassionate - and passionate about overcoming evil. We seek to save that which is good, which means we also seek to destroy anything that is evil." Colin's mouth had fallen open and he was gaping at Grayson.

Grayson frowned. "That is a disgusting habit," he said. Colin clamped his mouth shut.

Grayson sighed. The boy was totally lost. Perhaps he had given him too much credit for being astute. "We. Are. Wizards." He said it slowly, enunciating each syllable and looking directly into Colin's face.

Colin's eyes widened. "You're a *wizard*?" he gasped.

Grayson looked exasperated. "*We*," he emphasized, pointing at Colin and then himself several times, "are wizards." He heard Quant's muffled, but disgusted snort up in the rafters but chose to ignore him. He didn't need an owl to tell him that he was botching the boy's introduction to wizardry. He could see that very well for himself.

Drawing in a deep breath, he started over. "I am a wizard. I am three thousand three hundred and seventy-seven years old - quite young for a wizard really."

Colin slanted a look at Grayson's graying hair and the lines in his face but said nothing. He thought a great deal, however, and was extremely doubtful that any mortal man could live to be one hundred years old, let alone thousands of years.

Grayson didn't notice and went on. "I practice good, not evil." He shifted his position and thought for a minute before going on. "Your mother came to me some time back to tell me that she thought you might be a wizard as well. We began watching you, and while there were some very minor indications of differences between you and the other boys your age, there was never anything to make us truly conclude that you were different *enough*."

He gazed at Colin. The boy's demeanor had changed remarkably. Gone was the child's face; replaced with an angular, handsome face that was almost, but not quite, manly. He was growing in confidence and stature. Grayson nodded. He would be someone to be reckoned with in the coming years. He smiled, "Until, that is, you opened the sanctum door." He stood and began to pace beside the table, Colin's eyes following him, back and forth, back and forth.

"You were right. I did lock you out." He raised his hand as Colin began to protest. "Or, at least, I allowed you to be locked out. You had shown me no reason to believe you had even one ounce of wizard blood in you, and the only thing left for me to do was to test you. I needed to know." He plopped wearily into his chair. "I was convinced I was just not seeing your potential in the right way. Anyway, when you opened the door, I knew for certain." He peered at Colin until he began to fidget. "No one but a wizard could've opened that door, even if he had managed to place his hand in the right position. You," Grayson poked him in the chest, "are a wizard."

Colin sat silently for a few minutes, the look of consternation on his face turning into a wide grin. "So," he began tentatively, "can I make eggs and milk appear without chickens or cows?"

A loud chortling sound came from overhead. Grayson willed himself to remain calm. Perhaps the boy still had a ways to go before becoming an active wizard after all. "We'll see," he said firmly. Of all the questions in the universe, he never would've thought that the boy would ask about eggs and milk.

This endeavor should be interesting. But while it was somewhat funny at the moment, he knew that it would become dead serious soon. Their land was threatened by some kind of darkness that he couldn't explain, and he was afraid it would only get worse. The boy would need to buckle down with no distractions if he were to play a part in Terrene's future.

Abandoning the lesson he had been about to teach, he said, "Come with me," and walked out of the magnificent room, closing and locking the door securely. He led Colin into a tiny alcove with only a table and two chairs. On the table were a massive tome, a lantern, and several small objects scattered about.

Grayson opened the huge book and got down to business. Tapping the book, he said, "This is called a grimoire. It contains many of the things wizards need to learn to be successful." He opened the book almost to the middle and showed Colin the five pages he wanted him to study. "You aren't to look at any other pages but the ones I have designated," he ordered in his sternest voice, his eyes boring into Colin's. "Do you understand?"

Colin stared at the book. "Five pages. Don't read anything else." He huffed out a breath.

Grayson sat down and motioned for Colin to sit.

"Wizards have a duty to mankind. We must use our power for the good of all the creatures in the world, and for the world itself. But we must limit our interference. Every species needs to learn to fight their own battles, solve their own problems - as much as possible. We must be wary in choosing the times that we need to intervene."

His eyes darkened. "Some wizards do not follow this creed and instead choose to use their magic to gain power for themselves. They do not care that their evil ways destroy and wreak havoc. They want power, and any method to gain that power is acceptable to them." His voice rose and Colin watched him in awe. Grayson saw his look, and when he spoke again his voice was calmer.

"You have a lot to learn, but if you really focus on your studies you will learn quickly," Grayson smiled. "Let's see how you get on today, then we'll know how best to proceed."

Colin nodded. He was eager to get on with it. But a little fearful, too. What if he couldn't do what Grayson desired him to do? He was just a boy and certainly hadn't had hundreds of years of practice. He knew nothing of wizards. On the other hand, how exciting would it be to spout spells and turn frogs into squirrels? Why he . . .

Grayson looked at him sharply. "Don't even think it." Laying his hand on Colin's shoulder, he said quietly, "Wizardry is serious business. I trust you to do right." His eyes narrowed. "But if you disappoint me, you will be disappointing your parents, also, and yourself. Not to mention the world." His gray eyes bore into Colin's eyes as he enunciated each word: "I will never allow dark magic to be practiced by you. Are you clear on that?"

Colin put all thought of frogs away and nodded. Though what frogs and squirrels had to do with dark magic he couldn't imagine. He turned his full attention to Grayson who folded his hands in his lap and sat as still as a stone at the table, eyes staring at the tabletop. Not a muscle moved. His eyes did not flicker or blink, and his chest didn't even rise and fall noticeably. Colin watched raptly.

Suddenly, all the small objects flew into the air and hovered about a foot off the tabletop.

Colin gasped inaudibly. He was frozen, not daring to make any sound or movement. His eyes stared at the objects in amazement. As suddenly as they had become airborne, they descended back to the tabletop, one of them settling into Colin's open hand which lay still upon the table. In a blink Grayson returned from wherever he had been and gazed at Colin.

"Focus," he said, "is imperative in order for a wizard to learn. It takes time to learn, but learn you must." He laid his hands on the book. "The pages I've assigned you to study will teach you how to focus. Study what the pages say and then begin trying to move that stone in your hand. Even an inch will do." With that, he smiled at Colin, clapped him on the shoulder, and left him alone with the open book and the stone.

Chapter Eight

Colin looked around the small room before tugging the huge book closer. Before Grayson had opened it, Colin had noticed that the book was bound in heavy brown leather, with silver clasps on the spine, etched phases of the moon along the edges of the cover, and a silver pentagram in the center. A band of metal protruded through the pentagram and surrounded the book cover so that it could be locked.

The pages were made of coarse paper which had thinned from much handling. Colin would love nothing more than to flip through the entire book just to get an idea of everything it contained. He quickly put that idea out of his head, however, before it could take hold, and instead began perusing the two pages open before him. As he stared at the strange words, they began changing in front of his eyes from an unfamiliar language to the language of Terrene. He blinked before returning his gaze to the words. Had he imagined those oddly written words?

"No, I did not," he muttered. He began to read. It wasn't long before the five pages had been read and digested. He sat back and closed his eyes, mentally reviewing the most important points of the text. First, he must calm his mind and free it of all extraneous clutter. He knew his mind was rarely calm, and he would have to work hard to overcome distractions. Next, he must focus his body's energy by visualizing his energy as an all-powerful force. He huffed out a breath. That might be a little challenging. And, last, the energy must be focused onto whatever he wished to move. In this instance, the stone that was now laying on the table in front of him.

Shaking his head and rolling his shoulders, he placed his feet flat on the floor and straightened his spine. He would emulate Grayson's trance-like state. He licked his lips, pushed his hair away from his face, drew a deep breath and let it out, and closed his eyes. His foot was tapping, and he stilled its steady beat on the floor. Visions were jumping around in his brain like so many frenzied bats. He willed them to stop. They didn't. He tried to slow them down and finally succeeded - to an extent. With fewer intrusions in his mind, he began to color each intrusion white.

"Errghhh!" His eyes flew open. He couldn't do it. As he was trying to talk himself into just giving up, the words on the page in front of him caught his eye. "Never give up," it said. Colin made a face at the page. "Easy for you to say!" he cried. "You're just an inanimate object!" He began to push the book away but stopped short when the objects on the table started sliding along the surface forming a word in front of him.

He cut his eyes around the tiny room, sure that Grayson had sneaked in and was playing a trick on him. There was no one. Turning back to the objects, he looked suspiciously at them before leaning forward and reading what they had spelled. RELAX – in all capitals was spelled out before him.

"Huh!" he fumed. What in the world did they think he had tried to do? He swept his hand across the letters, sending the objects skittering. Before he could go off on a tangent about the whole idea of wizardry and focusing and anything else that came to mind, he stopped. He wanted to do this. The idea that he ought to be able to focus with just a modicum of effort was perhaps unrealistic. Conceited. Haughty, even?

Drawing in a breath that nearly left him breathless, he whooshed it out and relaxed into his chair, crossed his ankles, dropped his hands loosely in his lap, closed his eyes and began to envision some of his favorite things. As he focused on his mother's face, he found himself lulled into a sense of peace. Thoughts of home, swimming in the cave pool, walking in the garden, sitting on his perch on top of the world, the breeze whispering across his face, tending the horses with his father, watching the stars with Grayson. One serene thought slowly followed another. As his mind cleared, he saw a small fire in the center of his vision and focused all his energy onto it. He imagined a raging inferno, burning, burning, flames leaping higher and higher. Gigantic trees crashed to the ground. The heat and smoke were intolerable, robbing the world of its air. Explosive. The unremitting noise of the flames, like a million banshees wailing, devoured everything in their path.

Colin didn't realize that he was sweating profusely, but he was able to focus all that energy on the rock that he knew was in front of him.

When Grayson found him moments later, every object on the table was skipping around like leaves in a powerful gust of wind. As he watched, spellbound, the objects formed a unified line before settling gracefully back onto the table. The rock Colin had focused on remained poised in midair for a fraction of a second longer before dropping onto the tabletop.

As the rock landed with a small clunk, Colin opened his eyes. Eyeing the rock, he grinned. He had done it.

Grayson didn't move, not even to shake his head in wonder. But he did allow himself a huge grin, like a doting father, before masking his features. "Bravo," he said, coming toward Colin.

"Did you see that?" Colin jumped to his feet, the rock now in his hand. "I think I did it!"

Grayson nodded. "Yes, I believe you did."

"There was a big fire and I could see the rock through the flames. Next thing I know, it's poised in the air, and the fire's gone!" Colin exclaimed.

Grayson peered at the boy. He apparently didn't know the extent of his power. He didn't know that not just the rock that he now held, but all the other objects as well, had obeyed his command. He would be tired. This show of force from someone so young and unschooled was astounding.

"Come along and we'll get something to eat."

Colin led the way from the alcove. He still carried the rock; Grayson said he could keep it. He began to share all he knew about his experience before they had walked ten steps and was so wrapped up in the telling, he didn't see the magical book close itself and click the lock that bound it. Nor did he see the alcove vanish as Grayson followed him out, nodding along to his discourse, occasionally interrupting him to ask a question.

Chapter Nine

As the next few days passed, Grayson did not attempt to teach Colin anything new. "Practice focusing on small objects and learn to control the energy. Once you gain control, you may try larger objects." He started to walk off but turned back and said sternly. "Inanimate objects only!"

Colin grinned. He went about his chores almost gleefully as he used his newfound power to assist him. Before long, he could merely think about an object he wanted to move and where he wanted to move it and it happened. His gloves were summoned from the stone table in the garden. Vegetables floated through the air and into the waiting basket. Dishes stacked themselves on the table. Tumbled stones were stacked neatly.

One day as Grayson passed by, he noticed Colin glaring at a crow that had landed in a tree above him. He stopped. What would Colin do if he got angry? But Colin merely threatened the crow verbally with the frying pan if he ruined his fruit - just like he had always done - before turning back to his work.

As the end of the week approached, Grayson interrupted Colin's studies. He had continued to learn math, medicine, astrology, nature, and alchemy. They also still made their way to the rooftop most nights to gaze at the world above them, and they still practiced defense with their staffs. "Come. I have something I want to show you."

Colin looked at Grayson expectantly. Maybe he was to learn more from the Book of Magic.

Grayson saw his look and shook his head. "Let's go for a walk."

Colin needed a break and readily followed Grayson through the garden and then into the woods. The woods, if he remembered correctly, that he had been told not to enter. He was intrigued now and said nothing that might remind Grayson that he had been forbidden to go past the very edge of the woods. Grayson apparently read his mind, for he turned and said, "The only reason you are allowed this far into the woods is that you are with me. If I am not with you, then you may not go further than I have previously said. Is that clear?"

Colin scowled, but nodded his head. Grayson stood still while Colin remembered that nodding wasn't good enough for Grayson. He grimaced but said the words he would have to say if they were to continue. "I'm not to go any further into the woods than the boundaries you set earlier."

Grayson turned back immediately in the direction he had been heading. As far as Colin could discern there was no path as such, but Grayson looked neither right nor left as he strode forward. Colin was fascinated. Mossy boulders tumbled together in places, and giant trees whispered above him, their sound like music – or words. He listened intently but could make nothing definitive of the sounds. Some of the smaller trees formed elegant loops, and he stopped, spellbound, when he beheld a stand of trees, each formed in the shape of a heart. He heard rustling sounds, birdsong, and felt rather than saw movement among the trees from time to time. By the time they reached their destination Colin was convinced that Grayson was right in keeping him out of the woods alone. Not that he was scared. He wasn't. He just didn't think his imagination could be kept in check if Grayson wasn't there striding confidently along in front of him.

When Grayson spoke, he jumped and felt foolish for it. "Here we are," Grayson said as a tall, narrow building materialized right in front of their faces. The door, which resembled a puzzle with large broken pieces of glass as the puzzle pieces, opened before Grayson could knock. A tall, stocky, heavily bearded man in baggy pants, a long overshirt, and black boots, greeted them cheerfully.

"Hello, Peter," Grayson hailed him. "I've brought someone to meet you."

Peter peered down at Colin. "Have you, now," he smiled, returning his attention to Grayson. "I'm always pleased to make the acquaintance of such a likely looking boy."

Grayson placed his arm around Colin's shoulders. "This is Colin."

Colin reached to shake Peter's hand. "And, this is Peter," Grayson continued. "I think he might have some answers to a question you have asked more than enough times."

Colin looked doubtfully at Grayson. He asked questions all the time, so had no idea which question Peter might be able to answer. How could a total stranger answer any of the questions he had surely already had answered by Grayson? Grayson laughed and winked at Peter. "Do you have time to introduce us to some of your friends?" he asked.

Peter's eyes twinkled. "I always have time to show off my friends. Let me get my stick and I'll be right with you." He disappeared inside the house, reappearing in moments with a heavy burled walking stick.

"Come along," he called merrily as he began to walk through the mist that swirled around everywhere. The house was completely obliterated from sight when they had only taken a few steps. But in front of them a barn and several outbuildings became slowly visible as they walked closer.

Colin's mouth fell open before he remembered how disgusting Grayson thought that habit was and snapped it shut. He heard the chickens before he saw them. They were clucking and pecking around in a large enclosure close by. A magnificent black rooster twice the size of the hens strutted among them.

"Meet Gregor," Peter waved his hand toward the huge bird. Colin gawked at him. "Maybe you'd like to help gather the eggs later?" Peter asked. Colin nodded just to be polite, but he doubted he'd go anywhere near that enclosure as long as Gregor strutted within.

Peter and Grayson exchanged looks as Peter led them toward the barn. On the way, Colin was distracted by a huge wallow filled with all sizes and types of pigs. Most of them were quite large and sandy colored. Before he could get too interested in them, however, he caught sight of the most beautiful horses he had ever seen. They were large, with a distinctive gait, long flowing manes that flowed almost to the ground, and big, intelligent eyes.

Grayson stopped beside him as he stared. "Friesians," he said. "The most amazing and intelligent horse there is." He made a soft sound like a flute note and one of the horses raised his head and galloped toward them.

Colin was sure the horse was going to run right into them, but he pranced the last few feet, and stopped eye to eye with Grayson. "Hello, old friend," Grayson greeted the horse. The horse nudged him with his nose.

"You know me too well," Grayson said as he reached into his pocket and pulled out a perfect apple, letting the horse take it from his fingers. He rubbed the horse's neck as sweet apple juice dribbled between the enormous teeth of the horse.

Colin reached out tentatively to touch him but as the horse shook his great head, he snatched his hand back. The horse looked at him, nodding his head.

Grayson laughed and gave the horse a final pat before turning toward the barn where Peter patiently waited.

Though mist closed the barn in completely, there appeared to be filtered sunlight inside it that lit it enough that Colin had no trouble seeing the sturdy brown and white cows that stood placidly munching their hay. He shook his head. The milk, cheese, pork, chicken, and eggs he and Grayson devoured were apparently not magical at all. Peter let him pet the cows, which stood quietly as if unaware of the boy. "This one's a Dunlop. Her name is Tilda. Come right across here, and meet Hilda, who is a Guernsey."

Colin laughed. Hilda and Tilda. He wondered if all the cows had names that rhymed. Grayson looked on bemusedly as Colin lingered over the friendly cows.

Colin corroborated his theory that Peter furnished most of their meals with Grayson after they took their leave of Peter and made their way back home. As Colin glanced back over his shoulder as he walked beside Grayson it came as no surprise that the mist had closed the farm completely off from sight. He had a fleeting thought that perhaps the whole farm was an illusion that Grayson had created, but thought better of it. Grayson probably could make it happen, but Colin did not believe him to be deceptive.

"What about the fish?" Colin asked suddenly. "I guess Peter provides them, too?"

Grayson smiled. "Why, no, as a matter of fact. They come from another friend entirely."

Colin waited for him to elaborate but he just continued walking.

The days passed, with Colin gaining strength and skill. His mind and body grew. Yet he was still a boy, totally unaware of what life held for him, the challenges and responsibilities he was training for. He was content, and if he was a little puzzled by this new world of his, he embraced it wholeheartedly. If his fingers occasionally strayed to the small cross that hung from his neck, bringing his mother's face into view, that was neither here nor there. He understood that he was where he was meant to be. At least for now.

He saw the shadow twice more and as intrigued as he was, he still did not mention these encounters to Grayson. He did, however, try to find his way along the inner corridors to the bottom of the mountain to see what he could find. He was stumped by the only corridor that seemed to lead in the right direction. It appeared to lead nowhere, but he had too much experience with stairs that appeared and disappeared, secret doors, and rooms that faded away as if they had never been, to believe the corridor actually led nowhere.

He maintained a slight fear that a path would close off behind him and he would be lost in the bowels of the mountain forever. He was almost certain that Grayson could always find him, but the tiny doubt that remained kept him from being overly adventurous.

Chapter Ten

Aggie's long hair was pulled up and fastened on the top of her head. She had pinned it as close to her head as possible, using the pins she had had since childhood. She patted her hair to assure herself that all was in place and would stay put before pulling a nondescript skull cap over her head. She wore loose trousers that could be twisted and fastened at the calf, if desired, to tighten them so that they fit close to her legs. In close quarters and when fighting, the closer they fit the safer she would be. They were topped by a tunic that reached below her thighs but above her knees. She folded one of the cloaks Grayson had sent and placed it in her bedroll. It was made of a cross-woven material that protected the body like armor. It also had the added benefit of blending into all environments. If the sleeves were pulled over her hands and the hood pulled low over her face, she would become almost invisible, no matter the terrain she was in. Grayson had also sent Lucas a cloak, but they would save them for the more dangerous part of their journey.

The key that Grayson had sent was held on a chain around her neck. She had read the directions and had memorized the spell she would need to say once they arrived at the door deep within the Misty Mountains before burning the missive and scattering the ashes carefully.

Lucas was dressed similarly to her, and they both carried haversacks which they strung across their chests. Inside were various items they would need during their trip. All were essential, but the most important items by far were the cushioned vials of potions gifted to them by Grayson.

They left Bodun in the wee hours of the night two days after they arrived, careful not to be seen by anyone, and not mounting their horses until they were well away from the town. Alfred himself had opened a secret gate for them – one that was well-hidden and unguarded. There was no need for a guard because only Alfred knew of its existence.

They rode for days, not meeting anyone along the way, skirting the few towns they passed by several miles so there would be no chance of their being seen. If they happened upon any other travelers, their story would be that they were a displaced couple heading to Hernsart. They had now arrived at the topmost, tree-rimmed point close to the northernmost tip of the Great

Southern Plains. They had been fortunate so far and hoped they had not depleted their luck, for in the coming days they would need all they could summon - and cunning and strength – to survive. They would be leaving Fingal's Land and venturing into the Gehenna.

Once they were secure within the thick trees below the Misty Mountains they dismounted. They were exhausted and would rest for a day. The horses, Dahlen Ghea and Seig, stood quietly as Aggie rubbed their noses and ears, murmuring to them. With a final look deep into their eyes she whispered, "Falbh, mo charaidean," and watched as they faded from sight.

Lucas watched her for a moment before coming to stand beside her, his arm around her waist. "They will be fine with Peter."

Aggie looked up at him, tears threatening to overflow her eyes. She dashed the tears away and smiled. "I know. I was only wishing that we could've gone with them!"

Lucas grunted. "Yeah, it sure doesn't seem fair for them to be pampered by Peter while we spy on a bunch of bloodthirsty barbarians." They both sighed.

The next morning, they were up before the sun's rays had made it over the mountains. There was only a shadowy light, but it was enough for them to make out the main features of their surroundings. They made their way to the small creek near their campsite and quickly bathed several days' filth from their bodies. Aggie fastened her wet hair tight against her head once more before dressing in clean pants and tunic. She fastened the cloak at her neck, letting it hang behind her for the present. She wanted it close but did not feel the need for its safety features quite yet. Lucas did the same.

"Grayson said that once we reach the Tree Man, we will be near the opening that leads into the tunnels," Aggie reminded Lucas. "It should be slightly south of here."

Lucas nodded. "We are in the thickest part of the woods and once we walk south for a few miles the mountain should jut out right into our path. The Tree Man will be in that area." He pulled his compass from his bag and placed the chain that held it over his head, tucking it into his shirt. They slung their bags over their heads and across their torsos and headed south.

"We can forage along the way and save our other food." Lucas took the lead. They had already refilled their water jugs and would plan to refill them again in the cold streams within the mountain once they had found the entrance.

The narrow path they followed was barely wide enough for them to walk single file and was dim enough in certain areas that they had to gaze around them to pick it up again. Lucas checked his compass when they stopped, and they were mostly staying south. Though the path sent them meandering in a southwest direction from time to time, it always righted itself and turned back due south.

As they walked along, a smell floated on the breeze from the east, not overwhelmingly acrid or noxious, but just enough to make them pause and sniff the air. The scouts had mentioned an odor near the Gehenna. If they were getting whiffs of it from this side of the mountains, it must be strong indeed on the other side.

Otherwise, it was a beautiful day, pleasantly cool, with birds twittering away in the trees, and small animals scuttling along in the leaves on the forest floor. The trees were so immense and leaf covered that the sky was invisible in this part of the forest. The barely perceptible light from the early morning was still with them. Berries were plentiful along their route, so they ate their fill as they walked along.

As they got closer to the area where they expected to find the Tree Man, Lucas suddenly stopped short. Aggie saw the moment he stilled and stopped in her tracks, tilting her head to listen for any sound that might have caused him to stop. Neither of them moved, and Aggie realized she was holding her breath. Slowly and quietly she let it out. She thought she heard a slight clanking sound but couldn't tell where it came from. There was only the one tiny clank, then silence.

They watched and waited but heard nothing more. The usual common sounds of the forest had faded away. Cautiously, Lucas took a step into the brush close to the path and motioned for her to follow. The brush was tall and thick. They were completely hidden from sight as long as they remained still. For several long minutes they strained their ears to pick up any sound that wasn't a normal rhythm of the forest. They heard nothing more but thought it prudent that they remain where they were for a while. There had, after all, been attacks on a village near this area of the Misty Mountains.

They stood for what seemed like hours, until the forest sounds returned to normal. Squirrels and birds appeared in the trees overhead. A deer appeared beside them. Startled by their appearance, he quickly bolted across the path and away from them.

Lucas finally motioned for them to move deeper into the forest. They would give up their path for now. Perhaps they would be lucky enough to find another one, but he was disinclined to want to walk on a trail where others might be present. Moss grew thick under the canopy of trees and their footsteps were nearly soundless as they ambled east closer to the mountains.

They had lost a lot of time and still very little sunlight penetrated the trees. Mist hung in the air this close to the mountains, but it was thin for now and visibility was not impaired. When it began to grow darker, they made camp in a hollow near a tiny spring. Lucas took first watch, then slept as Aggie took over.

The next morning, they left as soon as they could see the ground in front of them. As the trees thinned slightly, they were amazed to see that the bulge of the mountain was just a short walk from where they had slept. The Tree Man would be in the vicinity of the bulge.

"What exactly did Grayson say about the location of this Tree Man?" Lucas asked quietly.

"Nothing really." She scrunched her shoulders and looked around. "It must be something that is readily apparent or surely he would've given us more details."

Lucas gazed around, his eyes following the base of the mountain and then perusing the sides of the mountain further up. He saw nothing. The mountain was rocky with scrubby bushes sticking out in a few places. Where they were standing, at the base of the mountain, there were no trees. He turned to look back into the tree line behind him. Nothing.

While Aggie continued to gaze at her surroundings, Lucas walked to the end of the bulge and then began to navigate his way around it. When he didn't come back in what Aggie considered an over-abundance of time, she began to walk toward where he had disappeared around the jut of the mountain. As she bent to pick up a stout stick in case she needed to clobber anything with it, a movement nearby almost caused her to scream. However, she really wasn't the screaming type, *and* she now had a weapon in her hand. She raised it high above her head and was just about to swing it with all her might when she saw that it was Lucas.

She let out a rush of air, dropped the stick to her side, and narrowed her eyes at him. "That's a good way to get your head bashed in," she said grimly.

He nodded. "So I see. Sorry, I wasn't thinking." He took a deep breath. "Since my head is still attached to my neck, come let me show you what I found."

He reached for her hand, and she grudgingly let him take it. "It better be the Tree Man is all I have to say," she whispered loudly.

He grinned. "I'm pretty sure it is."

Chapter Eleven

She gasped when she saw it. A gigantic trunk nestled in the crook where the two mountains joined together. She had never seen a tree so massive. The mist had dissipated and as her eyes followed the trunk upward, she saw two enormous limbs, one protruding from each side of the trunk. Because of the closeness of the mountains, they had grown out just a few feet before turning up alongside the mountains. It gave the impression of someone beseeching, or placating. Not too far above the placating arms was a craggy face with hooded eyes and a gigantic leaf-topped head.

"Amazing, isn't he?" Lucas said.

Aggie nodded. "We're blessed today. I'd guess that the mist usually covers him up."

She went over to examine the side of the Tree Man that was nearest them. Giant exposed roots snaked along the ground, sometimes rambling over each other, and forming caverns below. This is what she needed to figure out. Somewhere among the roots was a secret opening that would lead them to the mountain tunnels and thence to the Gehenna. Gingerly, she began to explore the area, making her way slowly around the wide girth of the Tree Man.

Apparently, she had started at the wrong side. She was more than halfway around the trunk and had found nothing. The back of the Tree Man was flush with the mountainside and she could go no further. She was afraid she might have missed the sign she sought and examined the tree more closely as she made her way back around and then to the other side. Surely it could not be at the unreachable back side of the monstrous tree! She shook her head. Grayson would've known if that were the case.

Suddenly, she stopped. She had almost reached the impenetrable back side of the Tree Man on the far side when she found the sign she sought. Rather than opening the door, she went back to tell Lucas.

They walked back into the shadows of the forest. They would wait until dark. Even though she didn't relish going through an unknown door in the dark, she also didn't relish giving away the location to someone who might follow them and do them harm.

They sat down on a fallen tree, out of sight, and dug into their small store of food. Their water would be replenished in the tunnels, but they would have to forage for food along the way. They still had enough to last them several days if they ate wisely. They heard nothing but the ordinary sounds of the forest, but they continued to speak in hushed tones, or not at all. They could watch the Tree Man from where they sat. If there had been someone in the forest earlier, he was gone. Or lying in wait? They could only hope for the former – and be extremely careful.

Finally, they roused themselves and Aggie headed toward the far side of the Tree Man. Lucas followed her from a distance as quietly as a shadow and found her holding a tiny pinprick light up to the tree.

"Here goes nothing," she whispered. Lucas tensed. He had no idea how all this worked and just hoped the ground wouldn't open up and swallow them whole.

"Open now and do it fast, open now and let us pass," Aggie whispered the words as she shined the tiny light on the sign scratched into the trunk of the tree, shocked as the earth opened beneath them and swallowed them whole.

There was little sound, just a barely audible whoosh as they were swept beneath the colossal tree. They landed with a thud below.

Lucas marveled that the fall hadn't harmed them in any way. "At least we fell in this soft grass instead of on solid rock," he marveled as he stood.

"Uh, Lucas," Aggie was staring at something large and probably dangerous coming towards them.

"Arrghh!" Lucas shouted as he grabbed Aggie's hand and took off running.

They didn't stop until they were out of breath. Aggie still held the pinprick light which had amazingly put out enough light for them to see, keeping them from endangering themselves even further.

"Grayson's idea of a joke, I guess," Lucas gasped.

They laughed until they thought better of the noise they were making. "Now that I think about it, it was probably just an oversized chicken that didn't appreciate us falling into his nest. Grayson wouldn't put us in harm's way." Aggie spoke low, but convincingly.

Lucas kept his thoughts to himself. No, Grayson wouldn't knowingly put them in harm's way, but that creature was no chicken!

"So, what now?" he asked, beginning to whisper once more.

Aggie shook her head. "The door that leads out of the mountain should be a ways from here. If there are tunnels that lead off from this one, the right one to follow should be marked like the trunk."

"I hope we don't have to be thrown down a hole into a giant horrible creature's nest again," Lucas joked. "What kind of marking are we looking for?"

"A witch's mark," Aggie replied.

"Oh, great!" Lucas blew out a breath. "Okay, let's go. I don't think we should talk anymore. All our senses need to be on alert."

Aggie nodded. "Let's be sure to find a place to fill our flasks. We need to fill them every chance we get so that when we get to the exit we'll have plenty."

Lucas retrieved one of the tiny pinprick lights from his pocket and took the lead. The light could be doused quickly just by folding it in his hand.

The tunnel was cool, but comfortably so. The air was fresh, not dank, though there was almost a wet forest smell to it. It curved around, sometimes to the right and sometimes to the left, but climbing steadily higher and higher for the first couple of hours. There were no side tunnels. At times the tunnel opened into cathedral-like rooms with gorgeous sparkling crystals glowing in the walls, arched walls with windows formed by stalactites, and dripping water trickling into the small pools that appeared often. They did not stop to fill their flasks until they reached a tumbling waterfall. This was sure to be clean water. They drank their fill and then walked on with full flasks.

Twice they found passageways where they had to choose which direction to go. Each time the witch's marks were scratched into the stone about three feet from the floor of the cave. If they had not known to look for them, the shallow marks would not have been easily noticed. The first time, it seemed the right thing to do to follow the witch's mark.

The second offshoot from the main corridor, however, was narrow and cramped. Even though the witch's mark clearly indicated that this was the way to go, they hesitated. It was dank and smelled of decay, stagnant water, and something far worse – a putrid smell that irritated their mouth and nose.

Lucas shook his head and mouthed the words, "I don't like this."

Aggie bit her lip. This did not feel right. Grayson had clearly written to follow the witch's marks, but could he have forgotten about this small passageway? She put her hand on Lucas's arm and motioned to move away from the smelly tunnel. They walked far enough away from it to be able to breathe clean air and stood speaking in hushed tones.

"I think we should keep to the main corridor. Surely, we're not intended to follow that smelly path," Lucas muttered, looking toward the disgusting opening.

Aggie followed his gaze and recoiled. What should they do? She opened her mouth to speak, but snapped it closed quickly. Lucas looked at her questioningly, but her raised palm and finger to her lips caused him to tilt his head to listen carefully.

Running feet. They looked wildly around. There was no place to hide, and if their ears did not deceive them, the noise was headed right towards them. Lucas grabbed Aggie's hand and took off the way they had come. As he went to pass the small, smelly passageway, Aggie veered them into it, dropping Lucas's hand so they could go single file. The passage twisted to the left and then the right, so they were able to keep the small lights lit. Their glow could not be seen unless the running feet pursued them into this arm of the passageway.

The noise was louder now, rhythmic and sinister in its intensity. Aggie was having trouble breathing in the putrid tunnel. She struggled to fasten a piece of her cloak over her mouth and nose as she jogged along, but the makeshift mask helped little. When she was sure they were deep enough within the tunnel, she stopped and melted into the stone wall, snuffing out the tiny light she carried. Lucas did the same as he stopped next to her. They both listened intently, but heard nothing. Lucas smothered a cough and fumbled with the catch of his haversack. He pulled out a handkerchief and handed it to Aggie.

Of course. Why didn't I think of that? She handed his handkerchief back to him and pulled her own from her pocket, tying it neatly around her lower face. They made perfect mouth and nose covers and while some of the smell still penetrated, the cloth helped keep them from retching.

They stood quietly, all their sensed alert. They had almost decided they had imagined the whole horror of being pursued when they heard a soft whisper of sound. Someone or some*thing* had hesitated outside the passageway they stood in. They strained their eyes in the direction the opening should be. Lucas silently slid his knife into his hand. They barely breathed. A slight clink sounded a step or two nearer. Had that someone or some*thing* entered the tunnel? It was as dark as a tomb.

Aggie's legs ached and she was terrified she would sneeze or cough or move and cause a pebble to shift. Even as cool as it was in the caves, she was drenched with sweat. With all her senses sharpened, the fetid smell seemed to have diminished somewhat.

Finally, the sound of whatever had stopped near the opening of the narrow corridor seemed to recede. Only the slightest whisper of sound, yet it was retreating, not coming closer.

They stood silently for many minutes until Aggie began to slowly edge further along the narrow path deeper into the cave, Lucas following closely behind. She wanted to get far enough into the tunnel so there would be no possibility at all of her light being seen, or any sound heard. After taking several cautious steps her foot reached out for purchase but there was nothing there. She began to fall and would have plunged into God knows what if Lucas hadn't grabbed her and heaved her backwards onto solid footing. Trembling, she clung to him for long minutes until her breathing settled back to normal. When she picked her head up from his chest, he immediately lit his light and, pressing her against the tunnel wall, motioned for her to stay put while he shined the light around.

The tunnel made a sharp turn to the left. Aggie had been following the curve of the wall on the right-hand side of the tunnel. Unfortunately, there was no wall on that side for about twelve feet. Instead, there was a three foot drop-off into a small alcove set away from the main path. She had become unbalanced when her foot reached into thin air, her body following.

Aggie lit her light and joined Lucas as he surveyed their surroundings. She breathed a sigh of relief when she realized she had been in no real danger. It was a needed warning to them both, however, that they must remain even more cautious than usual. Between the fear of pursuit and the fear of hurtling into an abyss, they had had enough excitement for one day.

Chapter Twelve

It wasn't long before Colin was given free rein to study the magical tome, the Grimoire, on his own. The unwieldy book was moved with great ceremony to the Enchantment Room and placed on a well-used, yet well preserved, wooden table so it could be easily read. A cushioned stool was provided for Colin, and he could often be found, elbows on table, chin propped in his hands as he studied the pages one by one.

As he matured, he became an exceptionally avid reader and a serious, scholarly student. No matter what Grayson threw at him, his mind absorbed it, understanding even the minutiae that many astute students never grasped. Grayson spent part of each day with him in this aerie quizzing him about what he had learned and making sure he understood each concept well.

Colin felt, at times, his head was exploding with all the knowledge that was thrust upon him, but he was an interested student, and good, very good, at wizardry concepts. Grayson would not brag on him over much, but he was more and more impressed with Colin's uncanny sense of purpose, technique, and skill. The experiments they did rarely failed - neither Grayson nor Colin was satisfied with an experiment gone awry. They molded and tweaked, studied and planned, until any possibility of failure was inconceivable.

Only once did Colin dare to try and right a botched experiment without waiting for Grayson. He was quite chagrined when Grayson came dashing into the room after the explosion to find him with singed hair and sooty clothes. A rare burst of profanity from Grayson on taking in the bedraggled appearance of the boy, the cluttered table, and the charred rug made Colin even more flustered. But he knew he had no excuse so said nothing. After Grayson took a few breaths, he merely sent Colin to get cleaned up and then to set the table to rights, with Grayson watching sternly over his endeavors.

Grayson frowned at the rug and surreptitiously flipped his hand, making the charred circle disappear. Once everything else had been scrubbed, thrown away, or returned to its rightful place, Grayson scolded Colin roundly, not to embarrass him or upset him, but to ensure he never entertained any ideas of repeating his disastrous performance. Grayson had nothing to worry about;

Colin had learned his lesson. Grayson hadn't had to remind him that he was a novice, though that hadn't stopped him from doing so.

In time, Colin's lopsided hair became less noticeable, and if he had been a worthy student before, he became an exemplary one. Quant felt bad as he watched the boy go about his business every day. He should have noticed what Colin had been up to that day, but had momentarily tucked his head under his wing and snoozed. He wouldn't let up his guard again.

One day, as Colin bent over the Grimoire, Grayson sought him out.

"Take a breather," he said, walking over to a more or less uncluttered table and laying a bundle upon it. Colin was curious and went over to look at what he had brought. He hoped it was food, for he was starving. However, Grayson was not laying out a picnic, but some unusual objects that immediately piqued Colin's interest.

Grayson laid his hand on Colin's shoulder and said, "You have been doing excellently in your studies and are making admirable progress." He motioned for Colin to take a seat on the high stool that was next to the table. "There are several tools that every wizard depends on. I thought you might like to look at these to get an idea of what you might prefer for your own tools."

Colin's eyes widened. Did Grayson really think he was ready for his very own tools? "Sure," he breathed, not quite ready to get his hopes up.

"Each wizard must be satisfied with his choices because these tools are extremely important in our trade." He picked up a grayish blue stone that was shaped into a five-pointed star inside a circle and was held by a narrow strip of soft leather so that it could be worn around the neck. He pulled a similar stone from inside his tunic and showed it to Colin. "These are pentacles. They represent the earth and physical strength." He placed his pentacle back inside his tunic and placed the other one around Colin's neck. "You may have this one as your own, at least until such time as you wish to change it for another."

Colin couldn't imagine ever wanting another one. The one Grayson placed around his neck seemed to him, though he was certainly no proper judge of such things, to have just the right look and feel. "Thanks, Grayson," he said earnestly. "It's perfect. Splendid, in fact."

Grayson smiled and picked up the next object laying on the table. It was a knife. What Colin would do with a knife he had no idea, but it was a beautiful thing to behold. The blade was forged steel with a double edge, sharp and deadly most likely. Colin gulped. Its handle was formed from obsidian, deep black with a greenish glow. While he knew little of knives, this one's handle fit his hand well.

"This knife is called an athame," Grayson said.

"What's it for?" Colin asked, not sure he wanted to know.

Grayson studied him a moment before saying, "Self-defense for one." Colin paled. "And this," he added, hefting the knife in his hand and quickly casting a circle around Colin. The circle glowed blue, then purple. Colin stared, mesmerized, at the glowing circle around him. "Protection," Grayson said. "You may step outside the circle once it changes to purple, but no one or no *thing*, can step inside but you." He vanquished the circle and placed the athame into a sheath, handing it to Colin with a slight nod of his head. "We will begin practicing forms of defense other than the staff soon."

Colin thought it sounded like a good way to get hurt, but kept his thoughts to himself. He had a chance to examine the sheath as Grayson fiddled with some of the other objects in his bundle. It was black like the handle of the athame. There were several symbols burned into the leather – a wolf's head, a tree, and a full moon with stars surrounding it.

Grayson interrupted his examination to show him something else he had collected. He held a stick out to Colin. "This came from a fallen branch of the hazelnut tree that grows in the garden. Wizards must always choose a fallen branch to make his wand, rather than taking a live one from the tree itself."

As Colin examined it, Grayson continued, "This wood is strong, yet pliant, and will do well." It was about fourteen inches long and similar to Colin's staff, though of course, much smaller.

Grayson showed Colin the amethyst stone and a clear quartz crystal which would be twisted into the end of the wand and fastened with copper wire. "I want you to make your own wand. It will belong to you and only you when you are finished. Once it is completed, decide what you would like to write on it, and I will write the runes on paper so that you can inscribe it into the wand."

Colin scratched his head and perused the collection of wand-making materials. Grayson left him to his thoughts.

While Colin had never made anything like a wand, he had seen Grayson's wand occasionally – Grayson was extremely protective of it and kept it out of sight when he was not using it. In fact, Colin did not know it, but a wizard's wand must never get into the hands of another wizard and, when not in use, Grayson turned his wand into another object so that no one would recognize it as a wand.

Colin had also seen pictures, and he had his staff, of course, to go by. He went to work, and when he had finished he had fashioned a wand that he was very proud of. Grayson was also pleased with it, but checked it out completely before beginning a lengthy discussion on how to use it.

"What would you like to carve on it?" Grayson asked, after he was satisfied that Colin understood the basic functions of his wand.

Colin answered without hesitation. "Wisdom and honor."

Grayson nodded and set the runes for the words down on paper for Colin to copy. "The Grimoire contains the ancient runes, and you may learn them at your leisure. For now, however, since there's so much more you need to know, don't use your regular study time for that."

Once Colin had inscribed the runes on his wand, Grayson led him in blessing the wand by first passing it over a pool of water and then over a burning candle. Salt was then sprinkled over its length. Colin now had three of the four tools he would need. He knew that the fourth tool was a chalice, though he couldn't imagine how a chalice could be useful in any way.

Days went by without Grayson mentioning the missing tool. Colin mixed potions without further mishap, cast spells, some of which worked while others didn't. He learned to tweak them to make them work and was more and more often successful. He continued his studies in alchemy, mathematics, history, astronomy, physics, and all the rest.

Grayson was true to his word and began to teach Colin the intricacies of fighting with his knife (using a wooden facsimile, Colin was happy to note) while continuing the daily practices with their staffs. He never came close to matching Grayson as a worthy opponent, but didn't expect to. His skill grew, however, and he thought he would be able to hold his own against lesser adversaries.

He began wearing his athame in its sheath, easily accessible to his right hand, and carrying his staff with him, along with the pentacle which always hung around his neck next to the cross his mother had given him. Colin thought of his old life often and missed his parents, but this new life was more than most boys could even dream about, and he was in his element.

As time marched on, Grayson introduced him to the bow, and they practiced every day with it, their staffs, and the athame until Colin was skilled in the complexities of all three.

Quant was resigned to the boy's presence by now. As Colin spent more and more time in the Enchantment Room, Quant moved closer to him. First, from the dragon's head to its massive foot. Then to the tops of bookcases, and finally one day he flew down right beside Colin as he studied. Colin raised his brows at him but then went right on studying. Quant sat nearby quietly staring at him with those golden eyes. It was almost discomfiting to Colin at first, but as he got used to the proximity of the huge bird, he began to enjoy his company, occasionally talking to him or reading his lessons aloud. Colin had a habit of muttering to his lessons as if they could hear – "you've got to be kidding", or "that can't be right", or even "how in the world am I supposed to learn all that?" He began to make those comments to Quant sometimes, with a shake of his head or a roll of his eyes, but he got little to no reaction from the owl.

One day Colin pushed the Grimoire aside and decided to practice telepathy on Quant. He focused on communicating a short thought to Quant without success. Though he strained to communicate almost daily, he hadn't received one word from the fractious owl so far. Still they stared at each other, Colin concentrating on sending Quant a message with his mind. Colin had no way of knowing that Quant understood him perfectly, but was just ignoring him. The old owl thought most things came much too easy to the boy and was testing him to see if he had enough fortitude to continue trying.

If there was one thing Quant couldn't abide, it was an arrogant, cocky boy. After a while, he had to admit that the boy wasn't really arrogant; he was in fact quite studious and curious. And if most things seemed to come easily to him, well, perhaps that indicated a brighter brain inside his head than Quant had been willing to acknowledge.

One day when the rains had kept Colin at his studies longer than usual, Grayson came in. In his hands he held a lustrous, dark silvery goblet, double rimmed in gold at the top. Colin's eyes lit up at the exquisite object.

Grayson smiled as he placed the chalice next to Colin. "For you," he said, stunning Colin. He reminded Colin that the chalice was the last tool that he needed in order to become a true wizard.

Colin beamed. "It's beautiful!" he exclaimed. "Wherever did you get it?" He began to examine the chalice without waiting for an answer. Between the double rimmed gold etching were runes that he could not read.

"It says," Grayson read, "water gives life to everything."

Colin nodded as he traced the cross that was etched into the chalice above the base. It also was gold. Twirled around the base of the chalice and onto the bowl of the chalice itself was a fearsome dragon. There was no other adornment, and Colin thought it the most magnificent thing he had ever seen.

He set the chalice aside and launched himself into Grayson, taking the older man by surprise. He coughed to cover his emotions and said, "You shouldn't startle a wizard so." He smiled down at the boy. "We have a tendency to react somewhat hastily when knocked about." Colin grinned up at him before stepping back a step.

"And to answer your question," Grayson said, "I made your chalice. While it's not really a birthday present, I thought your thirteenth birthday would be a suitable time for you to receive it."

At the look of awe on Colin's face, Grayson tut-tutted. "A wizard's chalice must be a gift. This chalice is my gift to you." He touched the head of the dragon and followed it around in a spiral to the tip of its tail on the base of the chalice. "The dragon is a symbol of good luck, heroism, supernatural powers, wisdom, and the circle of life. The spiral that is formed by his body represents your journey through life. A spiral also symbolizes your connection to the watcher of the universe and the energy that the universe contains."

Colin rapidly blinked back tears. Grayson had done all this for *him*. And had remembered his birthday. Colin hadn't even remembered that today was his birthday! He was overcome by such a wonderful and powerful gift.

Grayson sat down so he would be eye level to Colin. "You are about to begin a remarkable journey. Too soon, I'm afraid." He glanced at Quant. "But then, we don't usually get to choose what life throws at us. We only get to choose how we respond to it."

He tapped the rim of the chalice. "You now have all you need in order to prepare for that journey, and when the time comes you will be ready." He blinked and stood up, his hand resting on Colin's shoulder. "You will always have help. Never doubt it."

As if on cue, Quant stared at Colin until the boy returned his stare. "We will stand together when the time comes."

Colin heard the words in his mind as clearly as if they had been spoken aloud. Shocked, he stared at the owl, then at Grayson. Grayson smiled and then gave a brief nod toward Quant.

"You spoke to me?" Colin whispered. He was overjoyed. Quant had spoken to him. Perhaps that was his way of saying Happy Birthday.

"Thank you." Colin sent the message silently to the owl who might have nodded. It sure looked that way to Colin.

While Colin was involved with Quant, Grayson laid a round fig cake that he had drenched in a thin, sweet syrup next to him. It had thirteen candles on it, and with a snap of his fingers the candles were lit. He poured a tiny splash of wine in Colin's new chalice and a larger splash in his own, and holding up his chalice to toast Colin, he wished him health, longevity, and happiness. Colin grinned, then promptly choked on his wine. After Grayson had pounded him on his back far too many times Colin thought, they celebrated. Even Quant enjoyed the fig cake, though he couldn't imagine anyone enjoying wine.

Colin had never clogged his brain with so many words and new concepts. Telepathy. Psychokinesis. Telekinesis. Aura. Visualization. Spell casting. Energy. Alchemy. Enchantment. Potions. Incantation. Focus. They all had numerous parts, so the whole of what he was learning was almost staggering. Nonetheless, each and every day the concepts involved in wizardry began to take shape and become another piece of his increasing knowledge.

Colin was aware, though he was growing in stature, strength, and maturity, he was still a boy, but as each day passed his mind became sharper, more strategic, and shrewd. He practiced and studied and thought – and learned more than he ever imagined there was to learn in all the world. As he progressed, he became a more worthy opponent to Grayson, though he certainly wasn't fooled by his absolute inadequacy when faced by such a gifted and powerful adversary. His knowledge and skill, in fact, were mere pebbles compared to the mountain of knowledge and skill that Grayson possessed. He had not yet seen Grayson unleash his full capabilities, but imagined them to be unmatched by anyone in the universe.

One night as Colin stood chopping vegetables from the garden for their supper and Grayson was intent on grilling fish over the fire, the aroma of the fish reminded Colin that he still had no idea where the fish came from. They continued to appear on the cooking stone regularly, but from where?

"So where did you say our fish comes from?" He knew that Grayson had never said where they came from, but he *had* said that Peter did not supply them and had hinted that he would show Colin where they came from eventually.

Grayson glanced at him before turning back to the fish and expertly flipping them over. "I don't believe I ever said," he answered, annoying Colin, who rolled his eyes before going back to chopping.

"What's the big deal about where the fish come from? Is it some kind of Society of Old Wizards secret or something?" Colin said irritably, swiping his hair out of his eyes.

Old indeed! Young whippersnapper. Grayson snorted.

"If you must know," Grayson smirked, "it *is* a top secret of the Society of *Venerable* and *Elite* Wizards. Never heard of that society you just mentioned, but I will say that the true society does not share our knowledge with just anyone!" He laid the crusty fish on the trenchers as Colin humph-h-h-ed loudly and began to wield his knife even more fiercely on the vegetables.

"Don't look so glum," Grayson said jovially as Colin added the vegetables to their trenchers and plopped onto his cushion. "I'm not trying to be difficult, but I can't easily explain where they come from. . ."

Colin grunted and looked darts at Grayson until he thought better of it and lowered his eyes to his food.

Grayson sighed. "You didn't let me finish," he said. "I can't *explain* so you'd understand, but I can show you – that is, if you can get over your crankiness quite soon."

Colin snorted. "I'm not cranky! You baited me and you know it!" But he knew that he was indeed cranky, so made an effort to calm down. Silence loomed as Grayson left him to stew in his own thoughts. His bad moods were few and far between, and as predicted, it was only minutes before he was back to his usual congenial self.

He chewed his food thoughtfully. Grayson was right. A wizard couldn't afford to lose his control at all, let alone over such a small annoyance. He had felt his fingertips tingle as he had stared angrily at Grayson. Not that he thought for one minute he would or could hurt Grayson. Colin himself would be the loser, of that he had no doubt. Anger could end up costing him, or someone else, dearly.

Grayson admired Colin's spirit and perhaps he really had provoked him just a bit. But, nonetheless, he had a lesson to learn. Pushing his empty dish aside, he leaned on the table and peered intently at Colin.

"You must learn to guard your face and your words as though your life depended on it. A smile may buy you a fraction of time, where a frown or ill-spoken words may cast you into trouble you cannot escape. When you can, you need to walk away from a fight."

Colin had stopped eating and was watching Grayson. When Grayson was sure that he had understood what he was saying, he nodded at the boy and said, "Finish your meal and then reflect on what I have said. You may practice control on me, and if everything goes smoothly the rest of the week, we will go at week's end."

Chapter Thirteen

The dragon sat on his haunches, his eyes on the arched entrance as if expecting their arrival. Colin gasped. The black dragon's immense head with its startling blue eyes watched their approach. Even sitting, and Colin had never considered dragons at all, let alone one that could sit, the dragon towered over Grayson, who was taller than most men, making him seem insignificant in comparison. His arrow shaped tail draped over the boulders, circling half of the enormous, cathedral-like cavern. His scales were iridescent, green, blue, and purple. Two horns curved from the top of his head and his wings lay folded neatly at his sides.

The walls and ceiling of the cavern were studded with shimmering crystals and all the spires that dotted the perimeter of the cavern were the palest shade of blue. It looked like what Colin imagined a great cathedral to be.

A cascading waterfall plunged into a pool at the far side of the impressive room but there was no sound of water splashing. The water foamed and sprayed but was silent and tranquil.

Grayson strode toward the mighty dragon, seemingly fearless, and greeted him in a language Colin did not understand. The dragon appeared to smile, his gigantic teeth glittering in his mouth. Colin kept well back against the wall, not wanting to be anywhere near those massive jaws.

Suddenly, the cavern was enveloped in a thick fog. Colin melted into the wall behind him. What was happening? And where was Grayson? He held his breath, not daring to make a sound.

In a few seconds, surely less than a minute, the mist began to dissipate, and a man walked towards Grayson with outstretched hand, greeting him like an old friend. He was dressed as Grayson and Colin were – dark pants with a lighter colored belted tunic, and high boots. A pouch was slung over his chest and a sheathed dagger was attached to his belt. His hair was as black as a raven's wing, wavy, and reached past his shoulders. He was Grayson's height, perhaps an inch shorter, and his eyes were an even more startling shade of blue than those he had seen in the dragon's face. The stunning color of the forget-me-nots that grew on the side of Grayson's Mountain in the spring. They shimmered as though they contained extra light within them.

Colin blinked his eyes, then rubbed them. While he knew he was looking at a man, what happened to the dragon? He was nowhere to be seen, like he had vanished in the mist.

He stepped forward when Grayson motioned for him. "This is Simon Nilrem," Grayson introduced the man to Colin. Draping his arm around Colin's shoulders, he said, "And this is Colin."

Simon smiled and reached out his hand to shake Colin's. "Grayson has told me a great deal about you. Welcome to my humble abode." He winked at Grayson.

"Simon is our fisherman, in case you haven't guessed," Grayson said to Colin.

Colin *hadn't* guessed. His mind was more on giant dragons that disappeared and the splendor of Simon's *humble* abode than lowly fish.

Simon waved him towards what Colin had thought to be a soundless waterfall, but as they neared it, he could hear the pleasant murmur of the water. "Grayson tells me you're interested in knowing where your fish come from!"

Colin fell into step beside him, though his interest in fish had seriously abated. Was the dragon really gone? If so, how? Was Simon actually a dragon that could somehow change into a man? While it seemed far-fetched . . .

"I am, in fact, a dragon," Simon interrupted his thoughts. He looked wryly at Colin. "Sometimes, like when I have visitors, it's just more convenient to be a man." He stepped up onto one of the boulders that rimmed what Colin realized now was a sizeable lake, and held a hand down to Colin, pulling him up beside him.

The water rippled below, and Colin looked down to see hundreds, maybe thousands, of fish darting about its depths. It didn't seem particularly deep and was so clear that Colin could see to the bottom from where he stood. He recognized perch, trout, whitefish, herring, and salmon swimming nearby.

"Wow!" he grinned.

Simon handed him a net. "Why don't you catch your own supper today?"

Colin accepted the net and aimed for a large rainbow trout swimming close at hand. He lost his balance and began to tip over but was prevented from a swim by Simon grabbing him in the nick of time.

Simon laughed. "Go again, but this time move the net slowly into the water. Chances are the fish will swim right in."

Colin took his advice and deftly began to lift the net after a salmon darted in. Before he could remove it from the water, he had scooped up two more fish. Simon helped him land the heavy net. "That's enough for a plentiful supper and more!" he congratulated Colin.

Simon handed the net down to Grayson and then stepped down from the boulder, lifting his hand up to Colin after reaching solid ground.

Grayson caught Simon's eye over Colin's head. "Maybe this ought to be the night that you learn to cook fish," he suggested to Colin.

Colin nodded his head happily. "Aren't they beauties?"

A smile tugging at his lips, Simon said, "Tell Grayson you will cook them if he will gut them."

Colin blanched. He had never actually watched Grayson prepare a fish for cooking, but gutting one sounded like a terrible thing to be a part of.

Simon noticed Colin's paleness. He could never relate to some humans' reluctance to gut fish. He, after all, ate them whole most of the time – head, gills, scales, *and* guts. He smacked his lips at the thought, but quickly remembered that Colin was not a dragon, so was most likely more squeamish than he was.

"Don't worry," he said. "You'll get the knack of it quickly. Just think of the finished product, golden and crusty from the fire."

Colin nodded, but still wasn't convinced.

Colin and Grayson soon took their leave from Simon with a promise to visit again in a few days.

As they entered the serpentine tunnel that would lead them home, Colin asked, "Is Simon the one that makes the shadowy path across the Plains?"

Grayson considered a moment before answering. "In a way, yes. His human name is Simon, but his dragon name is Phantom of the Sky. It is, of course, his dragon form that flies." He peered at the boy, whose brow was furrowed in thought.

"It's all a little complicated, but suffice it to say for now that they are two very separate entities, not the same at all. When Simon is in dragon form he is Phantom of the Sky and lives a dragon's life. When he is in human form, he is Simon and lives a human life."

Colin mulled over what Grayson had said as he trudged along beside him. "Is Simon a wizard when he's a human?" he asked, curious.

Grayson shook his head. "No, he's not a wizard. He's a fisherman. More of a fish supplier, I guess, though he has other jobs."

"Like what?" Colin asked as they reached the last curve in the tunnel before reaching home. The light here became less dim than the twilight they had been walking through.

"Well, let's see," Grayson scratched his chin. "He's a seer. A wonder worker. A teacher at times. A warrior." He glanced at Colin.

"Huh," Colin muttered. He had never heard of a seer, or a wonder worker. And right now, he was losing interest because his rumbling stomach told him he was quite hungry. Instead of worrying about seers and wonder workers and dragons that turned into humans he began to worry that Grayson might make him gut their supper tonight. As hungry as he felt he just *might* be able to do it.

Chapter Fourteen

Aggie and Lucas huddled within the scant protection of a small basin which had most probably been an animal wallow at one time. The depression was deep enough for them to remain well hidden if they stretched straight out. It was roomy enough to even have a little wiggle room, and it was high enough up on the side of a hill to be concealed from anyone who might pass below them.

Their dark cloaks blended into the rocky land around them, and their faces were shadowed in the deep recesses of the cloaks' voluminous hoods. The sleeves hung over their hands and with all their skin covered, they were for all intents and purposes invisible.

They slowed their breathing, ears trained on the rhythmic sound of marching feet below, not daring to make a sound. Thankfully, the marchers passed by without incident and slowly the sound of their feet clomping along receded.

The two intruders into the Gehenna lay unmoving as the minutes ticked by, long past the time the troops could no longer be heard. Lucas thought that perhaps as many as twenty-five men were in the unit. He finally began to raise his head to peer over the side. A slight sound of falling pebbles caught his ear and he quickly lowered his head back below the rim of the basin.

Aggie had not moved, and he lay back down beside her, clutching his knife underneath his cloak, and straining to hear anything out of the ordinary. They lay long minutes but heard nothing. Still, since it was so close to dusk, they would not chance moving until they were shielded by total darkness.

The Gehenna was different shades of dark at all times, and as beautiful as some of the landscape was, in an other-worldly way, it was reputed to be quite dangerous.

There were muted browns and purples, the deep gray rocks, and more vivid reds, blues, yellows, greens, and oranges blanketing the landscape. They had never imagined anything like it. It was not lush; far from it. Instead, it was heavily eroded, and vegetation was quite sparse. The beautiful colors came from the sedimentary layers of the flat-topped mesas which looked like gargantuan tree stumps felled by some giant creature. Jagged obsidian chunks lay thick over the ground in one place, appearing like a wide river flowing through the land.

The two pools they had passed so far had bubbled and smelled strongly of sulphur. None of the water had been potable, which is what had put them on the path they had been following.

A spring with fresh clear water was close by, according to Grayson's map. Without that map it would have been a fool's errand to have entered the Gehenna. As it was, their water supply was low, and according to the map, the places to obtain drinkable water were at a minimum here.

When the gray light that hung over the Gehenna during the day turned to a deeper shade of gray they crept out of their lair. The deep shade of gray would morph into an impenetrable black soon. They would like to make it to the water supply before they were stranded in total darkness.

The map showed an obelisk standing a little apart from other boulders that were strewn across the small area surrounding it. They soon found the obelisk, but Lucas didn't like the setup surrounding it. Troopers like the ones that had marched past them earlier, wild animals, snakes, or a host of other malevolent creatures could hide in the nearby rocks and attack them as they neared the obelisk.

They crouched behind a stubby bush, taking note of their surroundings and the path they would take, and waited. The sky at night was like the sky during the day in one regard. A fiery orange burned against the blackness. The difference was in the totality of the darkness. Days were always hazy, but the shades of gray differed. There was no sun, so even with the fiery sky, there was never a bright, sunny day. Never a blue sky. And only a mix of gray and black clouds looming like a mighty storm. Even the fiery sky, patchworked by dark, threatening clouds, could not sufficiently light up the land below to simulate a normal daytime.

When the gray deepened to charcoal and they hadn't seen or heard anything, they slid on their bellies to the obelisk. The spring was on the opposite side from the boulder side according to the map. Once they reached it they lay still, listening, and slowing their breathing. Lucas glimpsed a scattering of tiny green plants right in front of his eyes as he lay next to the stone base of the obelisk. Water would be there.

Slowly, he began to dig down through the gravelly soil with his hands. Less than a minute later he felt the moisture. Soon there was enough water in the small hole to fill their flasks. He filled Aggie's first and handed it to her. She drank her fill while Lucas filled his flask. He then drank his fill before refilling both their flasks and their spare with the clean water.

They covered the spring back up with gravel, making sure they left no trace of their visit. Their approach had been over uneven rock, as would be their departure route. Unless they were extremely unlucky, their trail would not be visible to anyone passing by – unless he was scouting.

It was pitch black by the time they had gone less than a mile. While they would have liked to put more distance between themselves and the water hole, it was too risky to be stumbling around in the dark and they didn't dare to light one of the tiny lights. As little light as it gave off, the glow would be visible for a great distance. In this unwelcoming land, there were no stars, no moon, no campfires, or lit lanterns. Even so, they couldn't count on being alone.

They sat with their backs against a smooth stone wall. They would take turns trying to snatch what little sleep they might be able to get and would leave as soon as the gray began to reappear. They were nearing the wide corridor on Grayson's map that ran between an expanse of barren hills. The map was very old, but, so far, the sites marked on it had been just where they were supposed to be. Perhaps their luck would hold.

In this scorched domain, it was still hot at night. Aggie was exhausted. The silence they had to maintain was trying, and the danger that might lurk around every corner made her jumpy. Sweat glowed on her face and ran down her neck and back. She ignored it. The less she moved, the safer they both would be. Lucas was able to maintain stillness with little effort, but she had to focus on it every minute. If she dropped her guard, it could be a death sentence for them.

It was silent. No birds fluttered. No small animals stirred about. No insects droned by. No breeze swept by to whisper over their motionless bodies.

At long last, the dark night grayed. Their eyes adjusted to the changing light and swept the area thoroughly before they moved. As much as possible they stayed behind whatever sparse cover they could find. They made no sound as they walked. Soon they saw the ledge that would be one side of the corridor they would follow for almost thirty miles. Between them and the ledge was open territory. They knew the drill. Lucas would start out first at a jog. After counting to twenty, she would follow. Their weapons were at their fingertips. They were both fast runners. They surveyed the open land and didn't hear or see anything.

Lucas had almost made it into the cover of the ledge, Aggie not far behind, when an air-rending clamor exploded around them – behind and to Aggie's right. She darted a look, not breaking her stride, and paled considerably; her heart thudded, and the heat that had enveloped her turned to ice. As she threw herself behind the ledge, she heard the terrifying creatures, for they could not be human, galloping closer. Lucas had jerked out one of the precious potions in his haversack and was fumbling with the cork in the tiny vial.

Aggie snatched it from him and tore the cork out with her teeth. Quickly, she swallowed half the contents and thrust it at Lucas. He swallowed the rest quickly and almost before he could stow the vial in his pocket, they both began to fade from sight. He spied a crevice in the rocks and pulled Aggie into it just as the creatures rounded the corner of the ledge.

Lucas and Aggie scarcely breathed. The creatures were half naked with matted hair and a foul smell. They looked human in a grotesque way; some of them moved about on all four limbs while the others crouched about on two legs. Scared as she was that some part of her might still be visible, or that the fearsome creatures might hear some faint sound or even smell them as they hid, she couldn't help staring at them in revulsion. Suddenly a chill ran down her spine. There on the ground was the tiny cork she had spat out in her hurry to become invisible. She had broken one of the most vital rules of safety. She had left evidence as to her presence.

The sub-humans sniffed the air but apparently caught no scent of the two intruders hidden close enough to touch. They searched about warily, grunting and motioning. One of the four legged creatures snuffled at the ground, but miraculously did not find the tiny cork. Any prints that Aggie and Lucas might have left outside would've vanished once they swallowed the potion, so at least tracks wouldn't lead to the crevice where they were concealed.

As quickly as they had come, the fierce creatures disappeared without a sound. After long minutes of silence, Aggie peeked outside the corridor. It was empty, but so quietly had the creatures vanished she was loath to trust that their way was clear. Perhaps she and Lucas were not the only ones with magic potions? It was a sobering thought and made her wish they could stay invisible the whole time they were present in this deadly place. However, the potion had side effects if used too often and might make them even more vulnerable than being seen. They had other options at their disposal which would help, albeit in completely different ways.

For now, they exited the crevice and listened. The potion was good for another few hours so it would be in their best interests to make tracks while they were still invisible.

They saw nothing but the vast nothingness that was a part of this environment. They noticed the parallel ledge opposite them so knew they were in the corridor on Grayson's map. They could not see each other because of their invisibility, but Lucas whispered to Aggie to stay close to the ledge as they walked. Aggie reached for him, but her hand fell on empty air. She picked up a small flat rock near the ledge and was surprised that she could wrap her hand around it. She held her hand out in front of herself and, sure enough, she could see the rock floating in the air. Lucas apparently understood what she was doing, for suddenly another floating rock appeared near her own.

Despite the bleakness of their situation, Aggie grinned. They could tell where the other was as long as they held the rocks and stayed close.

Lucas's rock made a forward motion and moved away from her. She followed close behind, keeping within reach of the ledge. They had close to thirty miles of corridor to traverse before their real hardship began. She sent up a prayer to keep the demons away.

Chapter Fifteen

Grayson stared intently at the crystal orb he held aloft. He tried not to notice the tinge of creeping shadow that had begun to form inside one tiny portion of the lower surface of the ball. It was an evil portent, and he had hoped against hope that it would just go away. It had not, for as he turned the ball slightly, there it was, as persistent as ever. He expelled a breath and sent the orb back to its space in the rafters – out of sight, but by no means out of mind.

The threat was no worse, no better, so far. Even so, he believed evil was moving ever closer. And his feelings were seldom wrong. A chill ran through him. Simon foresaw it, also. A deadly war across the whole of Terrene.

Quant flew to his side. "I will plan to go to the border lands tonight. What do you want me to do once I get there?"

Grayson regarded the owl wearily. Quant was an excellent spy and an even better friend. He would prefer he not go at all, but Phantom of the Sky could not breach the space above the Gehenna without being seen and Quant could. "I would not ask you to go, old friend, if I had any other choice, but I'm afraid I'm out of options at the moment."

"You may trust me to be careful. I am happy to go. Just tell me what you would have me do." Quant blinked at Grayson, awaiting his orders.

Grayson chuckled. The owl had impressive powers which would help keep him from harm and he was certainly wise beyond his age. "I do trust you, as well you know. I won't say that I won't worry, even so." He drew a deep breath. "Aggie and Lucas are somewhere within the Gehenna. If things have gone according to plan, they should be nearing the Cauldron. You will need to check on them if it is safe to do so. They will be needing food, and you can make sure they have found the water sources I marked on their map. It not, you can lead them to water."

Quant nodded towards the rafters, "What of the shadow?"

Grayson shook his head. "That is worrisome. It appears to be coming from between the Derryveaghs and the area around the Cauldron. Lucas and Aggie will be headed to the western edge of the Cauldron and are not to go any further east than that. It's much too dangerous." He stared out the windows towards the Gehenna. "Heaven knows what is going on over there. But whatever it is, it's not good."

He turned to the owl. "Fly high and don't take unnecessary chances. Let Lucas and Aggie know what you find. Suggest to them that they head back across the border immediately if you feel it's necessary."

"I will leave at first dark," Quant said matter-of-factly. "Meanwhile, I will take a small nap."

Grayson nodded and began to fade from sight. "Wear your armor," he ordered as he disappeared from sight.

Quant smiled. Grayson was a complete worrywart.

In the garden far below, Colin was chattering away to Grayson while he worked as the older man leaned quietly against a fence. He had no idea the old wizard could be in two places at once, but it probably wouldn't have surprised him in the least. Strange things happened around Fearann Draiodh and that would be just one more subject he would insist on learning.

"Phantom of the Sky is going to take me for a ride," Colin announced, changing subjects so rapidly that the statement was almost lost on Grayson, who came to with a start as soon as it penetrated his brain. The boy had stopped what he was doing and was looking at him, his eyes imploring him to agree.

Grayson coughed. "When is this ride supposed to take place?"

Colin straightened. "Simon said that tonight the moon is full so I should be able to see well enough. He said it would only be a short ride."

Grayson quirked an eyebrow at him. "I don't think . . ."

"But he asked me!" Colin pouted. "And I already agreed."

Grayson studied the boy. Would he never learn? He motioned to the bench close by. "Come and sit down."

Colin dragged himself over to the bench and plopped down, his shoulders slumped.

"We have had this conversation before, but it will be repeated as often as necessary until you understand. You interrupted me without knowing what I was going to say, got angry, and pouted." He was pleased to see that Colin was abashed at this summation of his actions. That was a step in the right direction.

Grayson continued. "The fact that you agreed is neither here nor there. You don't have the authority to decide what you do and don't do. Input into decisions, yes, but not the final say." Colin squirmed and glanced at Grayson before looking away. "If I were a betting man, I would bet that Simon told you to ask me for permission before the ride would take place. Would I be right?"

After a moment, Colin nodded. "I'm sorry, Grayson. I really have been practicing listening and reacting appropriately. Quant has even been helping me." He lifted his chin. "I'll try harder, I promise."

"I know you will. You are still young, but the sooner you learn to control yourself, the better. Patience is something we all need more of. I'm not saying you'll never experience anger or frustration, but there are ways to react to your emotions without losing control. If, for instance, you listen fully to what someone is saying to you without interrupting, you might not end up being angry at all. Sometimes you might. But don't react until you have listened. Until you have understood, you have no basis for any reaction. Does that make sense?"

Colin nodded. "Yes."

"So, shall we try again?" He didn't wait for a response from Colin before saying, "I don't think your first ride should be at night, with or without a full moon. Dawn would be a safer time until you get used to sitting on a dragon. I will inform Simon that you will be waiting for Phantom on the Promenade before first light, appropriately attired and excited." He smiled. "Is that agreeable?"

Colin smiled back. "Thanks, Grayson."

If Colin had thought riding a dragon would be just a matter of climbing onto his back and holding on, he was mistaken. Grayson went over the correct way of mounting a dragon – over the wing – and that the only place to sit on a dragon is right behind his head in front of his wings. Since Phantom had great curved horns, Colin would be able to hold onto the base of these; otherwise it would require a strap of some kind fastened around Phantom's neck. Most dragons are not fond of a strap. But then, most dragons will never be ridden by a human.

Grayson also taught him to keep his knees and lower legs pressed lightly against Phantom's body. Not too tight, but just enough to feel secure. If, for whatever reason, Colin began to slip or lost his grip on the horns, he should press his legs in tighter and Phantom would know to adjust his position in the air to seat him upright again.

Colin blanched a little at the possibility of falling off and plummeting to the ground. Grayson saw his discomfort and said, "Don't worry, Phantom would never let you fall. Dragons are extremely fast and if you *were* to fall, not that you ever would, mind you, Phantom would catch you."

Then there was the armor. Colin was shocked when Grayson brought him the most beautiful set of armor he had ever seen. Grayson called the back and chest plates a brigandine. It was made of a triple layer of soft leather. Grayson assured him that even though it was supple and soft, it would stop almost anything from penetrating deeply enough to actually harm him. But the main reason he would be wearing armor was because of the wind and because of the extremely minute possibility of a collision with some object in space – a bird, perhaps.

"Better to be safe than sorry, I always say," Grayson repeated as he often did. He was a stickler for safety and planning for all eventualities. "These greaves will cover your lower legs and will be strapped over your boots." He held a pair of leather boots up for Colin to see. There was some type of design on the sides of the boots and Colin looked at them closely. The symbol had three overlapping, interconnected pieces with pointed ends interlacing a circle. He turned a questioning gaze to Grayson.

"What is that symbol?"

"It's called a triquetra. The circle is not always a part of a triquetra, but it symbolizes the circle of life, as we've talked about before. The triquetra itself is a very powerful protection symbol that protects you from harm." He said it matter-of-factly, like he was prone to do, but Colin knew that Grayson was a strong believer in symbols.

Next, Grayson handed Colin a helmet that fit close to his head and left his face exposed. Once he tried it on and found it fit, Grayson handed all of Colin's new equipment to him. "Place these somewhere handy for tomorrow's early ride, then meet me in the garden with your staff. You still have much to learn."

The next morning, long before the first light lit the land, Grayson and Colin were on the Promenade, Colin in full gear, awaiting the arrival of Phantom of the Sky. Grayson handed Colin a small bottle and bade him drink.

"This will make you invisible for a little while, in case for some reason you and Phantom are caught out in full light. Phantom blends well into the night, but unless he flies far too high for you to survive, he is quite visible in daylight, and you do not need to be seen."

Colin drank the few drops of liquid and began immediately to fade.

"Don't worry," Grayson explained. "You won't be completely invisible unless the dawn completely breaks. It's just a precaution."

Colin heard a soft whirring and Phantom appeared at the edge of Colin's perch. One wing poked onto the perch and Colin hurried over it and onto the dragon's neck, just behind his head as he had been taught to do. He reached out and grasped the base of the horns and grinned at Grayson, though the grin was barely noticeable in his faded state.

A deep voice spoke, "Are you ready, Colin of the Sky?"

Colin stared at the head of the dragon. Would wonders never cease? Phantom could talk! "Yes, ready," he said, his grin widening. He was riding a dragon!

Phantom swooshed upwards until they were soaring far above the trees and then over the vast Plains. Colin was mesmerized by the view from so high. The land was a miniature version of itself. He could see the Misty Mountains far to the east as Phantom zipped through the air. The mist over the mountains was thin, but suddenly thickened and closed the mountains from view.

Phantom circled and flew to the Cagar Mountains to their south. To Colin's delight he flew up and over the tall mountains. Colin got his first glimpse of the Sea of Mists, the mist that shrouded the water almost hiding the sea from sight. However, Colin could see specks of the turbulent aquamarine water below as they flew over. It was amazing! His eyes watered from the wind, and he was sure his cheeks were as red as poppies. He bent low over Phantom's back and gazed in wonder at all the sights below. He could get used to flying through the air on a magnificent dragon and wished he could do it every day.

He was disappointed when Phantom dipped and turned, heading back over the mountains, but the sky was beginning to lighten. It wasn't long before he was being dropped back at his perch.

"Thank you so much, Phantom of the Sky," he enthused, his delight quite apparent as he made his way back over the dragon's massive wing and jumped onto his perch. He waved until Phantom was out of sight.

"That was amazing!" Colin exclaimed as he caught sight of Grayson leaning against the wall. He pulled the helmet from his head, causing his hair to stand on end. He was less dim now, so Grayson could easily make out his features. His eyes were alight with joy.

"I'm sure it was," Grayson agreed. "It's not often that humans, or even wizards, get to ride a dragon. You should feel honored."

"Oh, I do!" he said.

As Colin elaborated on his ride, Grayson's mind wandered to the shadow forming in his crystal, and to Quant. He had not been able to search for him or Lucas and Aggie yet, but he would make time today. He felt a dreadful foreboding and knew that even if evil was not already upon them, it would only be a matter of time. Now was the time to act.

Colin noticed that Quant was gone the moment they stepped into the Enchantment Room. "Where is Quant?" he asked Grayson as he surveyed the empty dragons above his head.

"Even wise old owls have to take a vacation every now and then."

Colin studied Grayson, who was bent over his cauldron studying the contents with rapt attention. But he didn't question him further. Instead he got straight to his books and the concoctions they would teach him. He was used to Quant being there, but as the days passed and he didn't return, he acclimated to Grayson's more demanding personality. It was a time to prove that he had patience and control. He hoped he was up to the task.

Grayson and Colin worked harder than ever. Colin seemed to take on Grayson's urgency. There was little time for pursuing leisure activities. Instead, Grayson taught, and Colin learned. Colin was curious when Quant did not reappear in the Enchantment Room as days passed, but Grayson did not seem worried, so Colin did not question him.

By the end of a week, Colin had no further doubt that he was indeed a wizard. Grayson had insisted he was one all along, but until now he had not felt like one. He had gained immeasurable confidence in his power and had even passed muster with his new ability to listen totally and to react appropriately. Grayson was impressed and told him so.

On the last night of the week, Grayson had another surprise for Colin - it seemed his supply was never-ending.

As Colin sat beside Grayson near the fire before bedtime reciting his alchemy formulas flawlessly, he was startled by the appearance of an enormous furry beast padding toward him. It was the color of the forest – brown, gray, rust. With large ears that pointed forward and a long bushy tail hanging straight down. His eyes glowed amber. "Gahaaah!" Colin shouted, shrinking into his chair. His heart pounded and he froze into his chair, unable to retreat.

"Meet Olcan," Grayson announced, seemingly unaware that Colin sat petrified as the huge beast walked serenely over to Grayson and laid his massive jaw on his knee. They greeted each other like old friends as Colin stared.

Colin was shocked. Did the huge animal just nod at him? He shook his head. No way. Did he? His heart began to slow to an almost normal beat as the monster settled quietly between the two chairs. He figured the animal outweighed him by at least a hundred pounds, probably more, and couldn't imagine what might happen if he decided to take a bite out of him. "Does he bite?" he whispered to Grayson.

Olcan flicked an ear at Colin and Grayson chuckled. "I've never known him to eat anyone. It's probably best that we are both wizards, though. He gets along well with me, so maybe he will tolerate you, too."

Colin stared at the brute dubiously. "What is he? A bear?"

Grayson shook his head. "No, he's a wolf. A protector, a guardian, though I imagine he could get pretty fearsome under the right circumstances."

Colin leaned on the arm of the chair, his chin in his hand, looking down at Olcan. "He sure is big. Does he come to visit often?"

"He comes every night."

Colin looked at Grayson, surprised. "Why haven't I ever seen him before?"

Grayson puffed circles of smoke out of his pipe, then pursed his lips and puffed out a circle within a circle.

Colin grinned. "I didn't know you could do that!" he exclaimed.

"I'm a man of many talents," he winked. He laid his pipe aside and stood up. "Olcan's not much of a conversationalist, so he comes late. After you're in bed. Speaking of which, we probably need to turn in. We can finish the formulas in the morning."

Colin eased out of his chair. As he straightened to his full height, the wolf stood up and shook himself. Colin started, but then took a deep breath, and held his hand out to the fearsome animal. When he didn't get his hand bitten off, he stretched to rub Olcan's head.

"Come along, you two. Bedtime."

Olcan yawned widely, his gigantic teeth glinting in the dim light. Colin withdrew his hand and scurried off. Grayson banked the fire as Olcan watched, then followed him to bed.

Chapter Sixteen

Aggie had never been so glad to see anyone in her life than when she spied Quant on a boulder next to their camp. Except for his bright amber eyes, he blended perfectly into his surroundings. Aggie knew that he could hood his eyes to prevent them from glowing, but apparently he had scouted the area and didn't feel the need today.

She smiled at the great owl. "I'm so glad to see you," she whispered. She noticed the welcome pack of food below him on the ground and broadened her smile as he answered telepathically, "Grayson thought you might be getting hungry after your trek through the desert."

She grabbed one of the loaves of bread from the pack and broke it in two. She spoke telepathically, also - something she had learned from Grayson many years before but had had little use for until recently. "He was right. We ran low on food two days ago and have had to eat some rock-hard, weeks old, tasteless bread, and a few agave stalks we were very lucky to find." She bit off a good-sized chunk of the bread and gobbled it down.

Lucas stirred and shot straight up when he noticed Aggie was not beside him. Before he could start crashing about in alarm, she handed him half of the loaf of bread. He stared at it, then at her, and finally at Quant sitting serenely upon the boulder. He nodded gratefully to their esteemed visitor before sinking his teeth into the crusty bread.

"You found the spring?" Quant asked, still with his mind, not his mouth.

Aggie nodded as she communicated back, "I think we'll be fine now, thanks to this great food." She looked down at the overflowing pack of food. When she looked back up at Quant, she was startled to see a tiny sparrow sitting on the boulder instead of a great gray owl. She waved as the sparrow flew away. Quant could shape-shift? She hadn't known.

Lucas prowled silently around the edges of the camp. Everything seemed quiet and peaceful. If there had been danger, he was sure that Quant would have alerted them, but he still didn't take anything for granted and did his own assessment.

When he was sure that they were indeed alone and as safe as they could be in such a harsh environment, they divided the remaining food between their two haversacks. They had filled their flasks with spring water before going to bed the night before, and according to Grayson's map, they would find more fresh water within a few hours. He took a last look around the camp. While he hadn't been extremely happy to sleep on stony ground, at least there were no prints to wipe away. The pack that Quant had brought their food in had faded from sight as soon as the last of the food had been removed from it. When he was satisfied that they had left nothing to give their presence here away, he and Aggie shrugged their haversacks over their heads. They both had daggers in their boots and swords strapped to their backs. The potions were close at hand. While they would have liked to stay invisible for the rest of their journey, it wasn't safe. In most instances, their cloaks would be enough.

They traveled wordlessly and soundlessly, something they both abhorred, but it was necessary in this hostile place. Aggie would have said that being filthy and hungry were two more items she could add to her list of dislikes – if she had been allowed to talk. Thanks to Quant, she could mark being hungry off her list for the present.

Lucas led the way, and Aggie followed his broad shoulders through the dramatic pink, orange, and lavender undulating landscape that stretched for miles and would eventually lead them to their destination: the vermillion mesa that Grayson called the Sliabh Dearg. Here they would find water – and a secret passage through the mesa to the Cauldron.

The fiery sky gave off enough light to see during the daytime hours, but just barely. With the grayness, and the mist that sometimes shrouded the land, they blended into the landscape as well as could be expected. The up and down of the land, however, made them more likely targets as they topped each of the hills.

They hastened their steps, needing to get out of the open as soon as possible. Maybe lay low for the part of the day when they would be most visible.

After they had walked for a couple of hours, Aggie looked at the sky in front of them. It was still black and fiery, menacing. It was filled with giant spider holes. She was very wary of those spider holes. Did monstrous spiders live there? Did the holes allow evil somethings to come through them, or did the holes pull something up into them and devour them? She shivered. They were creepier than anything she had ever seen, and lately she had seen a *lot* of creepy things.

The haze that clung to much of the land they had traversed thus far today was vanishing. Amazingly, the smell of sulphur and decay was also beginning to dissipate. She thought it ironic that as they neared the largest bubbling lava bed in all the Gehenna, the smell and the haze vanished.

As they reached the top of one of the undulating dunes, they met an unsettling sight. The land flattened suddenly and in the flattened area grew mushroom-like trees sparsely scattered across the floor of the valley. Hundreds of large earthenware crocks lay tumbled about, some upright and some turned onto their sides with what appeared to be their covers flung nearby.

They froze and exchanged looks. Lucas unsheathed his sword. What was this? They both stared at the sight below, but they saw no movement, heard no sound but the wind, which made an eerie moaning sound as it howled through the trees and over the openings of the crocks, giving them pause.

Lucas finally shrugged his shoulders and sheathed his sword. Nothing seemed to be amiss, so they stood for a few minutes just reveling in the wind, their scorched skin welcoming the whisper of breeze over it. A few strands of Aggie's hair blew free from her tightly coiled knot and whipped at her face. She smiled at Lucas, tucking a strand behind her ear, and he smiled back. Except for the wind, it was still and quiet. They decided to stop under one of the dragon's blood trees for the day - for that is what the trees were.

Lucas headed toward the nearest tree, Aggie trudging behind him, when a flurry of activity exploded around them. Lucas grabbed his sword and Aggie's hand and ran. If they could make it to one of the trees they might be safe. The bright red resin of the dragon's blood trees was a powerful protectant. He gripped his sword harder but didn't turn to see what pursued them, sprinting at full speed toward the nearest tree instead. As he closed in on the tree, Aggie stumbled. He caught her up and flung her onto the ground beneath the tree.

As he sprung after her, he caught sight of a hideous looking creature closing in on him and felt a stinging in his left leg as of a hundred bees attacking. He swung his sword and opened a gash in the tree, wiping the resin from the sword over Aggie's prone form. Another stinging sensation and he toppled. As he fell, he swiped his hand on the tree trunk where the resin flowed freely like blood.

When he came to, he lay where he had fallen, between the tree trunk and one of the overturned urns that lay near the tree. As he lifted his head he was looking straight into the opening of the crock and was astounded to see that the hole did not stop at what should be the bottom of the crock, but continued tunneling into the ground. He threw himself away from the opening. The creatures that had attacked them must have come from the tunnels beneath the crocks.

His leg hurt like hell, but he had to find Aggie. His face contorted with pain every move he made but he managed to roll over, sweat beading on his face. The breeze, and the howling music of the wind were gone. Aggie should have been right beside him under the tree, but he couldn't see her. "Aggie," he dared to whisper her name. He saw his sword and grasped it, sticking it into the ground beside him and using it as leverage to work himself into a sitting position. His leg was killing him. He rubbed the sweat out of his eyes. At least he was alive.

"Gaaaha," he sputtered as Aggie dropped to the ground beside him.

"Eat this," she ordered, shoving a dried leaf bud into his mouth. He gagged and almost choked, but she moistened his mouth with water, so it somehow went down. It was extremely vile tasting."

"My leg," he moaned.

"Yes, I know," she said. "Eat another of these." She shoved another of the vile leaf buds into his hand.

"What *are* these disgusting things?" he asked as he placed it in his mouth and then spat it out without swallowing.

"Don't waste those!" Aggie admonished him. "They're leaf buds from the top of the dragon's blood tree, and they are all that's standing between you and an agonizing death." She looked darts at him before pulling another of the buds from her pocket. This time he choked it down without comment.

She started to pull off his boot, but grabbed his sword instead. She reopened the gash in the tree and drew a circle of the blood resin around them and the tree. She went back to his boot, tugged it off, and pushed up his trouser leg. The back of his leg was riddled with pinprick holes from his ankle to his knee, red, and already beginning to fester. She wiped the blade of his sword over the back of his leg and then smeared the resin over the lower leg as he watched. "What are you doing?" he asked. Now he looked bloodier than ever.

"The resin from the tree is called dragon's blood and is supposed to not only protect, but to ease pain and help heal wounds. I thought I'd give it a try." She rummaged through her pack, her mind filled with combinations of herbs that might help heal Lucas's leg.

"How bad is it?" Lucas gasped. If pain was any indication of how bad it was, it was really, really bad.

"It's not that bad," Aggie lied. "Just lie still." She couldn't tell if he had fever because their bodies were always hot in this blazing place.

She made a poultice of garlic, turmeric, and aloe vera and then added one of the concoctions from Grayson's store of potions. It was labeled WOUNDS, so surely it must be some kind of magical cure-all? Once the poultice covered the dragon's blood she had smeared earlier, she dampened a cloth with water and placed it on Lucas's forehead. Then gave him a cup of water to drink.

"Are you hungry?" she asked.

He shook his head. "Not right now." She took off her cloak, folded it, and placed it under his head. He closed his eyes and was soon fast asleep. She was worn out and just hoped that what she had done was enough. As she settled in against the tree trunk, she saw a form in the distance on top of one of the crocks. It was facing them, unmoving, but a threat if not for the safety of the dragon's blood tree. She smirked at the form and closed her eyes.

Two days later, Aggie's smirk was replaced by a furrowed brow and frustration that no matter how much she tried to focus on a positive outcome for herself and Lucas, she saw no way out from under the dragon's blood tree without dying. Their guard still remained, waiting for them to make a move. If she had thought he was their only foe, she wouldn't have been concerned, but she knew the others waited in the tunnels below.

They should've been at the mesa by now - and water. They were running low, and even though their food supply would last for days, thanks to Quant, it would do them no good without water. The dried figs had some water content but not enough to sustain them.

Lucas's leg pain was less now, and she had prevented an infection with the poultice, but he could not walk any distance. She had had such good luck with the poultice, she decided to examine the other potions in more detail and was excited to find one that would banish evil creatures. However, her joy was short-lived. In Grayson's neat handwriting, the label explicitly stated it could be used to banish *a* threatening creature. While only one creature was in sight at the moment, she couldn't believe he was the only one around. She felt sure the others would erupt from the ground if she and Lucas attempted to leave. If she banished the one guard, would that prevent the other creatures from being summoned? She shook her head. Just as she thought there might be a way out, two more creatures appeared and arranged themselves close by.

The invisibility potion was their only option, but there was still the problem of Lucas's leg. If they had to rest often and the trip to the mesa took longer than expected, they would need at least three doses each. That would be too dangerous.

Perhaps the hideous boar-like creatures wouldn't be able to follow them once they left the dragon's blood trees and the Crock Valley, but how were they supposed to do that with guards now surrounding them? They had no way of knowing how far their range was. If she and Lucas were invisible and managed to escape, would the creatures be able to follow them?

Any solution would be rife with guesswork and therein lay the danger. But she and Lucas would have to decide on a plan of some sort today.

When Lucas awoke, Aggie went to sit beside him, turning her back to the guard closest to them and examining their surroundings carefully, including the treetops. Nothing stirred.

"How is your leg?" she spoke quietly. She reached to pull his trousers leg up to check the wound.

"It seems better. Of course, I haven't tried to stand on it this morning." He closed his eyes and sighed. "We're going to have to leave soon. We can't wait until we're too weak to make our escape." He searched Aggie's careworn face. He could tell she was exhausted.

Aggie nodded. "We'll have to wrap the leg tightly before we go. That should ease the pain somewhat, keep it from jarring as you walk, and also keep your boot from rubbing the wounds." She removed the poultice and smelled it. It had no odor of infection and the wounds appeared to be healing.

"Why don't we leave the dressings off today and let the wounds dry a little?" She got up, went to the edge of the circle, and buried the poultice, sprinkling a powder over it that would eliminate any scent.

Lucas watched her as she returned to his side. He put his arm around her, and she nestled into his shoulder. "We will have to go, Aggie," he whispered. "No matter the consequences. The only choice we have, as I see it, is to go and fight if need be, or to lie down here under the dragon's blood tree and die."

She sat up and stared at him. He tucked a strand of hair off her face and smiled. "We are fighters, not cowards. All these pathetic brutes are babes in knickers compared to us. We just need to figure it out. Let's think of Colin. He is depending on us, and we cannot let him down. *We have a chance*," he stressed.

Aggie paled at the thought of her son. They would make the effort. She was determined to get back to him. She summoned her last drop of humor and said wryly, "Make that a *very slight* chance."

"No," countered Lucas, "make that a better than average chance." He reached over and kissed her cheek.

"We will leave tonight. Most of our stuff has stayed packed, but throughout the rest of the day, let's tidy up a bit – discreetly, so nothing will seem out of the ordinary. In the process of packing, we'll remove the vials of invisibility potion and each of us will carry a vial in our pocket, wrapped carefully so it won't be easily broken," he said. "We can slather resin over our clothes. That ought to help.

Yes, they would go. Aggie drew a breath, "I'll leave your leg exposed for now and then wrap it later in the day. We need to rest up, exercise your leg a little, and eat well." As she turned away, the thought suddenly struck her. If they could eliminate the smell of the poultices, why couldn't they use the powder to eliminate their own scent? The other creatures that had chased them seemed unable to smell them, but they were different from the creatures in the Crock Valley. Could they afford to risk their lives based on an assumption? Lucas thought they had no other choice.

Later, Lucas glanced around their circle, surreptitiously watching their guards. They didn't seem concerned about an attempted escape and apparently never had to sleep or eat, which was disturbing. He hobbled around the inside of the ring of dragon's blood getting his bearings. According to Grayson's map, they needed to head east out of the Crock Valley towards the mesa that would be visible soon after topping the hill that formed the eastern border of this valley. His gait was slow but not quite so painful as the day before. He would eat some of the buds and resin from the dragon's blood tree throughout the day, and with the resin dabbed over their clothes they might stand a chance.

As Aggie watched Lucas gazing beyond the boundary of the ring, she sensed a blur of movement out of the corner of her eye and jerked around. One of the "unconcerned" foes was not so unconcerned after all. With a low growl, big yellow teeth bared, he slunk towards them, his beady pig eyes red as he stared right at her from only a few feet away.

Lucas stopped and turned towards the sound. Though he knew they were safe within their circle, he picked up his sword. If the creature got close enough, he would reach outside the circle and kill him. But as the horrible beast stared at him, others came out of the tunnels below the crocks and circled the ring. His growl must have alerted them. They were growing impatient.

Lucas lowered his sword but did not put it down. He could not risk reaching beyond the circle with at least fifty of the creatures so near. One of them would love to tear his arm off.

Aggie had drawn her sword and came to stand with her back to Lucas so they were back to back and could see in all directions. Suddenly the creatures stopped growling and lay down, all eyes pointed in the captives' direction.

They all stayed frozen in position for more than an hour. When no further attempt to enter the ring was made, Lucas and Aggie strapped their swords on their backs and went about their plan, packing up a little at a time, eating, slipping the potions into their pockets, sprinkling themselves as discreetly as possible with the odor eliminator. They divided the last dribble of water between their flasks, packing away the empty third flask.

Aggie dressed Lucas's leg as the landscape began to darken a shade. He pulled on his boots, and they both drew their cloaks around them and sat down with their backs against opposite sides of the tree. The creatures seemed to have lost interest in them, but they knew that looks could be deceiving.

Lucas turned his head toward Aggie. "This is not going to work, even with the invisibility potion," he said quietly. She could hear the concern in his voice and her breath caught. "They're too close to each other. We have no room to walk between them, and I don't think even if we're invisible we can actually walk on top of them and get away with it."

Aggie sighed. She was at her wit's end. "You're right, of course. Maybe they'll just go away before too long."

Lucas shook his head. "Let's try to get a little rest. We'll just have to wait them out."

At some point they nodded off, and if they had ever had a window of opportunity, which they had not, it was gone.

Aggie started. She had heard a sound above her. She cracked her eyes open a slit and listened. She knew that nothing could penetrate the dragon's blood ring, could it? She had just about decided that she had been dreaming when a voice sounded in her head.

"Well, you seem to have gotten yourselves into a bit of a pickle," a voice she recognized very well said.

She grinned and nudged Lucas. They weren't going to die after all. Not this night at least. Somehow, Quant had found them when they needed him most.

"How did you know where to find us?" she sent the message up into the tree. She had pointed Quant out to Lucas with a nod of her head. He, of course, could not hear their conversation, but was happy to see the canny owl - he had no doubt that Quant would have a workable solution to their problem. That would make twice that Quant had rescued them.

"I had no idea," Quant said. "Grayson asked me to check on your progress on my way back home. He thought you'd be nearing the mesa, so I was headed there when I saw this disgusting pack of offal lying about" - he looked menacingly at the vile creatures surrounding them - "and decided to check it out."

Aggie was giddy with relief. "We're so glad you did. As you can see, we seem to be held captive."

"Not for long," Quant said. "Your rescue is being implemented." He turned his hooded eyes to Aggie. "I thought you and Lucas might want to hear about that incredible boy of yours while we wait."

Aggie choked back a sob at the mention of Colin but controlled herself quickly and whispered to Lucas about their upcoming rescue.

As she relayed Quant's news about their son to Lucas, they could barely contain their pride in everything Quant shared with them. Colin had flourished under Grayson's tutelage.

"He misses you both," Quant finished. "You can be very proud of him – though I know you always have been." He ruffled his feathers and stared into the sky before turning back to them. "He is the wizard you've always imagined him to be, Aggie. He is already a force to be reckoned with, though he doesn't understand that yet."

As Aggie relayed that information to Lucas they stared at each other with wonder as Quant turned to the business at hand. "Your ride is no more than two minutes away. Gather your belongings and move quickly and quietly to the easternmost edge of the ring. Sky Strike will hover low just long enough for you to jump on and will take you to the mesa."

As he finished, there was a slight thrumming noise and a colossal eagle hovered low to the ground, but did not land. The snarling beasts came alive, but backed away when they saw the size of the mighty bird. Aggie and Lucas quickly jumped aboard.

"Stay safe," Aggie heard, and grinned toward the spot she had left Quant. She blinked. Again, a tiny bird fluttered into the sky and was lost to sight.

They both relished their escape on the giant bird as they soared away from the snarling, angry beasts below. He was the largest and the strongest of all the War Eagles - ancient, colossal, winged predators that lived high on the cliffs overlooking the Sea of Mists where the Northern Mountains intersect the Derryveaghs. His wingspan was twenty-four feet, his height nearly eight feet, and because of his heaviness, he glided on air currents more often than flapping his wings, rarely landing on flat land.

One more danger left behind. How many more would they encounter? They were on the last leg of their journey. If they could get through the mesa tunnels and out the other side, they could scout the area around the mesa side of the Cauldron, and then head home. They had not found what they were looking for. A few fierce warriors and a colony of reeking, growling boar-like creatures could not possibly be the only dangers that they and Alfred feared came from this place. They had not encountered any of what they imagined the people of Gehenna to be. So, where were they? Perhaps the last leg of the journey would be the worst. She shuddered, took a breath, and made herself calm down. She would enjoy the ride - as quickly as they were traveling, their lost days spent underneath the dragon's blood tree would be made up this day.

Chapter Seventeen

The shadow had been spreading across the crystal like an epidemic. It was black as a starless, moonless night, and as tumultuous as a stormy sea. Grayson stared at it, his mind refusing to grasp the horror that was imminent. He watched the raging shadow for a few minutes. At least, for the moment, it seemed content to merely rage. It had changed very little in the last two days, but Grayson no longer doubted it would become more malevolent in time.

He replaced the crystal on the stand beside him and went to stand before the copper framed obsidian stone. Colin had thought it mirror-like and he wasn't wrong. However, instead of seeing images that reflected into it like a regular mirror, its dark surface was more like a window to the rest of the world.

As Grayson focused his mind on the Gehenna lands - particularly on the area of the Cauldron - the surface began to lighten and blur, then formed its window into the land of fire and darkness. As he waited, the picture began to grow sharper. His eyes widened and a grimace spread across his startled face when he saw the hundreds, maybe thousands, of monstrous beings before him. He looked steadily over the army of demons until a face appeared before him. He blinked and lost his focus for a moment. It was a face he knew – and dreaded. So shocked was he that he lost the image abruptly, the window slamming shut. But not before he saw the skeletal face of his old nemesis, Ben Toreke, looking straight at him and laughing, mocking him.

He hurried to the map of Terrene that took up one wall of the Enchantment Room, tracing his finger along the route Aggie and Lucas should have followed. If all had gone well, they should be within two days of the Sliabh Dearg. They must be summoned home. Quant, also, had not returned, and Grayson had been unable to reach him.

He tapped the area north of the Cauldron. He was reasonably sure this area was where Ben Toreke had stood, his goons of doom spread out around him. His eyes searched the map and lit upon Hell's Door. This fiery inferno within the Cliffs of the Ancient Cromlech was reputed to be the entrance to the Underworld. Grayson himself believed it to be. This was where he had cast Ben Toreke's evil body to eternal damnation more than 2,000 years before. If that despot had managed to escape, and to bring thousands of Death Reapers with him, his powers had grown tenfold: no, at least a hundredfold.

No time to think about it now. There was not a minute to lose. He hastened from the Enchantment Room through the corridors to the precipice of the highest cliff on Grayson's Mountain. Colin was in the garden. He would be fine for a while.

The wind was blowing briskly this high up and whipped Grayson's neatly tied-back hair into a frenzy around his face. He paid it no attention as he concentrated on intercepting Quant. No matter how his agile brain strained to communicate, there was no answer. Where was that owl? He scowled. It wasn't like Quant not to respond to him.

Perhaps he could reach Aggie. She was not as sensitive nor as practiced in the art of telepathy as Quant was, but it was surely worth a try. He sent a message. Nothing. If he didn't reach her or Quant soon, she and Lucas would be walking into a firestorm they would never be able to survive. If they left the relative safety of the mesa tunnels, they would be doomed.

He lifted his staff up towards the sky causing the wind to shift and form a funnel. He sent an incantation of protection softly through the funnel which carried his words high above the Misty Mountains. Whether they would carry to the Sliabh Dearg he had no way of knowing. He smiled grimly. At least he had made sure that not one of the Death Reapers or Toreke would benefit from his spell.

With Lucas, Aggie, and Quant out of reach, this was beginning to be a nightmarish day. He wished he could just lay down somewhere and close his eyes, but instead he rushed off the cliff, through the corridors and back to the Enchantment Room. He grabbed up the crystal from its stand and was astonished to see that the shadow was inching forward.

"Olcan, come," he telepathed urgently. The wolf was beside him in minutes. Grayson greeted him with a pat on the head as he quickly wrote out a note.

"Olcan," he said as he placed a collar around the wolf's neck, the message folded inside, "I need you to take a message to Hagan of Hernsart. Find him at night when he is alone. He will know you carry a message from me. When you have delivered the message, gather your friends on the Cosmic Caverns Tundra and await further instructions."

He rubbed the wolf's head and looked into his eyes. "The situation is getting more desperate every hour, my friend. You must go quickly."

Olcan took him at his word and vanished.

Grayson wasted no time but went straight to Phantom of the Sky's lair below. As he entered the crystal cave, he saw Simon, glad that Phantom of the Sky was already in human form, which would make communication a bit quicker.

"I sensed there was something urgent going on and have been waiting for you to arrive," Simon shook Grayson's hand.

"You are right, as always," Grayson said, his serious demeanor giving way to a half smile for the briefest of moments.

"It has begun," he said as Simon showed him to a nearby bench where they both sat down. "The Gehenna is over-run with demons straight from Hell."

Simon started, then shook his head, "But Grayson," he exclaimed, "Death Reapers cannot escape their doom. The Underworld does not release anyone from its fiery pits." He stopped and stared at Grayson as understanding dawned. "You've seen them, haven't you?"

Grayson let out a heavy sigh. "If I had not, I would never have believed it." He hesitated for a moment. Looking straight into Simon's eyes, he added, "Ben Toreke is leading them. Somehow he has escaped his fiery grave and has brought thousands of reapers with him."

Simon jumped up and began to pace, his dark hair rippling in the slight breeze that he stirred up as he marched up and down the space in front of Grayson. Grayson wished he had the energy to join him.

Suddenly he stopped, his face tense. "What of the Gehenna people? They have always kept to themselves, though I know of the rumors that they are the marauders that have been raiding Fingal's Land."

"I saw none of them near the Cauldron. They have either joined forces with Toreke, gone into hiding in the tunnels, or been slaughtered." His face darkened as he thought of one more possibility. Could Toreke have figured out a way to cast the Gehenna people into the flames in exchange for the Death Reapers he took out? It didn't bear thinking of.

"I need you and Phantom of the Sky to rally the dragons in the Land of Frozen Waters. We also need the elves, ice fairies, and snowbirds to join us if you can convince them of the probability that Terrene will be destroyed if we do not join together in unity."

Simon scoffed. "I'll talk to Apricity and will do my best with the others. The dragons will join, of that I'm sure."

Grayson nodded. "Yes, we can be sure of the dragons," he smiled wryly at Simon.

Simon shrugged. "Shall I summon Sky Strike and the rest of the War Eagles?

"Yes. Then check that the entrances to the mountains from the Gehenna to the Land of Frozen Waters remain blocked. Have everyone ready themselves for war. If Toreke attacks, it will probably be from the area of Hell's Door in the Cliffs of the Ancient Cromlech. He can invade Fingal's Land and The Land of Frozen Waters from there." Unlikely though it would seem to most inhabitants of Terrene, who knew little of wizardry, the Cliffs would be one of their staunchest allies.

"Phantom and I are prepared to go. We will leave immediately." Simon always spoke as if there were two entities going rather than one, and in some ways it was true. But while he and Phantom were indeed two very different creatures, only one could be present at a time.

"Give Apricity my regards and tell her I am in her debt."

Simon nodded. "I will deliver your message and will have everything in order when the time comes."

Grayson hurried toward the garden. Colin would be wondering where he had got off to. He had a plan forming in his mind as he approached. Colin was standing propped on his rake, staring at the long row in front of him. Weeds were scattered about between the rows where he had thrown them as he yanked them out by their roots.

Grayson halloed him. "Those weeds are not going to jump out of the middles by themselves," he said. He half-thought that Colin might be trying to conjure them out without benefit of the rake, but the boy turned towards him, smiling.

"Just resting a minute."

Grayson surveyed his work. He had accomplished quite a lot. "Why don't you call it a day? Go on and wash up and spend a bit of time at your studies until it's time to eat."

Grayson watched as Colin waved and then sauntered off, placing his rake next to the wheelbarrow before entering the cavern. Only then did he walk towards the tree where the Great Horned Warrior Beetles lived. He whistled three distinctive notes under his breath and waited.

Soon Commander Scarabee poked his head out of a tiny hole in the bark of the massive tree and ambled onto a limb near Grayson's head. He was the same beetle Colin had locked into his tiny fort months before - and continued to search for from time to time, even though he rarely was able to find him.

"Hello, Wizard," the Commander said in a voice that was more of a squeak than the commanding tones one might expect from a mighty Commander. It didn't matter, of course, because he was the only one of the beetles that could speak at all. Beetles communicated in other ways, but Grayson had insisted that the Commander be able to speak if needed, so had placed a spell on him. While Grayson could communicate with any creature or plant, there were times when Commander Scarabee carried messages to those who could not, and only at those times could the Commander speak in whatever language was appropriate for that single purpose. "I hear you've got a bit of a commotion on your hands," he squeaked, his curved horn swaying as he talked.

"News travels fast," Grayson said, his shrewd eyes examining the beetle.

Commander Scarabee coughed a small barking cough. Perhaps it was more of an embarrassed laugh, come to think of it. "Well, ah, you know how it is. Some of my comrades are not content to stay at home and mind their own business and would rather roam at will. While they can't talk, they *can* communicate." He backed up a bit as Grayson scowled.

"Oh, don't worry," the Commander hastened on. "They're all quite loyal."

As Grayson continued to stare at him, the beetle clapped his tiny mouth shut.

"Don't worry about it, Commander," Grayson said genially. He would have to cast a spell to keep those nosy miscreants inside their own territory. Not that he doubted their loyalty, but privacy was essential to a wizard's work.

Changing the subject, he continued. "I need your help, Commander."

It was the beetle's turn to look shrewd. "Of course, of course," he said speculatively. "What can I do for you?"

"I am sending the boy to take a message to the Abbot at the Forgotten Abbey, and I would like for you to accompany him."

The great beetle shook his head as if he were a bull instead of a tiny beetle! "What on earth for? I can't be a nanny to that boy!" Looking at Grayson's grave face, he backed down a bit. "I mean, I know you must have your reasons, but why me?"

Grayson assured him that he would not be a nanny. "I need you to be his bodyguard."

Commander Scarabee blinked. "I see," he said slowly. "What might I be guarding him from? The Friars are formidable fighters but are allies of ours last I heard."

"Yes, they are great friends," Grayson answered, stroking his beard. "The boy, Colin, is smart and powerful and is well on his way to becoming someone to be reckoned with. But he is still a boy, and I must say, a little reckless at times - though he is working admirably to contain that recklessness," he hastened to say. "I need someone I can trust to see that he comes to no harm."

The Commander swelled with pride at Grayson's acknowledgement of his loyalty and prowess and put aside any further objections he might have had. He stood as tall as his small body would allow and snapped a salute to Grayson. "You were right to come to me. I will be honored to be of service. Just inform me of my duties and I will not let you down."

Grayson laid out his plans. "You and Colin will travel underground through the Cagars, exiting where the Misty Mountains intersect. There you will climb the narrow staircase Colin will unlock which will lead you to the exit onto the Abbey rooftop. You are to ask to speak to Abbot Tomas Fergus Galloway. Colin will carry a letter for him from me. It cannot be given to anyone else."

"I see," the Commander said, his great horn quivering. "I will agree to that," he added after he had thought about it for a moment.

"Do you have any questions?" Grayson asked.

"We-e-l-l," Commander Scarabee said tentatively. "I do have a couple." He ambled closer to Grayson, so they were eye to eye. "Firstly, am I to travel in my present form?" At Grayson's nod, he continued. "Then I must have a suitable means of transportation," he said importantly. "I refuse to ride inside a pocket or any other degrading conveyance for a beetle of my standing."

"Go on," Grayson's face remained placid. "Any other requests?"

"Yes, one other thing," he cleared his throat. "I must be in charge. I will not take orders from a mere slip of a boy."

Grayson reassured Commander Scarabee that he would have transportation that befitted his station. "Perhaps you would have no objection to riding atop the brim of the boy's hat? There you will be able to scout the area easily, you will be at the same height as he is, and you will be able to communicate with him, if need be."

The great warrior thought about it and could find no objection. "That should suit," he agreed.

"Splendid!" Grayson smiled at the beetle. "Also, let me just say that if you feel the need to metamorphose for any reason, you may feel free to do so."

The Commander nodded as Grayson continued, "As to your second question, there should be no doubt that you will be in charge. I will make sure that Colin understands that. However, I have a small request of you."

"Yes, of course," the squeaky voice replied.

"I would like for you to pretend that you and Colin are a team and, when possible, to make decisions that are agreeable to you both. Colin needs the practice, and you can always reject any of his decisions that you deem inadvisable. There really should be no decisions to make as the journey will be very straightforward."

The beetle sighed. After a moment of silence, he huffed out, "Very well."

Grayson breathed a sigh of relief when all the particulars had been worked out. He admired the Commander and his army of beetle warriors, but he had no more time to dilly-dally.

He found Colin with his head still in his books, though from the looks of things, he had not kept his head there continuously. Ignoring the clutter, he asked Colin to take a break. They needed to talk.

Grayson had debated how much of the threat to divulge to Colin and had decided to keep only to the role he would play in the unfolding drama for now.

"I've got a job for you," he announced. He could tell by Colin's quizzical expression that he was torn between jumping at the chance of a possibly exciting job, and being highly suspicious of exactly what kind of job it would turn out to be. Not to keep him waiting, Grayson delivered his request immediately and matter-of-factly. "I need a courier, someone I can depend on and trust, to deliver a very important message."

"I'll do it!" Colin exclaimed eagerly, his face alight, not waiting to learn any of the details.

"Don't get ahead of yourself," Grayson admonished. "You need to know what I'm asking you to do."

"Oh, okay," Colin sighed. He managed to listen quietly, only his bouncing foot and widened eyes giving away his growing excitement as Grayson droned on. He already knew what his answer would be, of course, so when Grayson completed his narrative about the proposed mission, he replied just as enthusiastically as he had before, "I'll do it!"

Grayson shook his head. He hoped he wasn't letting the boy take on too much responsibility. The journey should not be dangerous if Colin followed the plan, but what if he got sidetracked? Surely, Commander Scarabee would be able to keep him in check.

"I am sending Commander Scarabee along with you. You and he should manage just fine."

Colin squinted his eyes at Grayson. "Who?"

"Commander Scarabee," Grayson repeated. "You've met him before. He is a famous warrior who has earned a reputation and more medals on the battlefield than most soldiers could ever hope to see." He grinned inwardly. He thought he'd leave the beetle on the hat part until it was actually unfolding.

"I don't remember meeting him," Colin replied, his brow furrowed. "I think I'd remember someone like that." He turned questioning eyes to Grayson.

"Well now, ahem, I think you might recognize him when you see him." He changed the subject back to the mission before Colin could quiz him anymore.

"You and Commander Scarabee will go as my emissaries to the Abbey That Time Forgot. The Abbey is located in the Valley of the Forgotten Abbey."

"Figures," Colin muttered.

"What was that?" Grayson asked.

Colin shook his head. "Nothing."

Grayson continued. "To reach the Abbey, you will have to travel through the underground tunnels of the Cagars to the intersection of the Misty Mountains. Once you arrive, there will be a stairway that will lead you almost to the top of the mountains. You, and no one else, will be able to see a door as you near the top. Be looking for it so you won't miss it. It is a secret exit onto the rooftops of the Abbey. You will ask one of the friars to take you to Abbot Tomas

Fergus Galloway. Once you have been taken to the Abbot, you will deliver my message and then you and the Commander will follow the route back home again. No tarrying. Come immediately back. Do you understand?"

His piercing eyes studied Colin. "Now, repeat what I said." Colin was used to this process, so repeated the gist of the mission back to him until Grayson was satisfied.

Grayson nodded. He would give Colin the message he was to carry right before he left, written in runes so that only the Abbot could decipher it. He had decided not to give the spell that would unlock the door to Colin. Only two people knew about the door or how to unlock it, and for now that would remain. Colin would be able to see the door because Grayson made it so. He would be able to exit through it because Grayson would see to it. He would also then forget where it was because Grayson would make sure of that, also. For now.

"The Commander will meet us in three hours in the tunnels below. The tunnels are exceedingly hard to navigate so to you it will look like there is only one tunnel, while in reality the tunnels are labyrinthine, much like a warren. If you were to get lost, no amount of conjuring will help you escape. The Commander will see all of the tunnels, but he will not try to steer you away from your set course. Follow the tunnel right in front of you and you will be safe. This is very important. *Do Not Wander in the Cagars*! Do you understand?"

"Yes, at least I think I do." Colin bit his lip, an anxious expression on his face.

"Don't worry," Grayson smiled. "It will all make sense once you begin." He stood. "Come. You must rest. I'll prepare food for you to eat before you leave and some to take with you. You will need all your wizardly accoutrements, so go ahead and gather them up. I will awaken you in two hours." Grayson put his arm around the boy's shoulders. He would do fine.

Chapter Eighteen

Colin never thought he would sleep, but he did. After a hearty meal, they were on their way to meet Commander Scarabee. Grayson went over the main points of the trip once more in what Colin thought was so excruciatingly detailed that he might doze off at any moment, but as Grayson continued to remind him, "It's better to be safe than sorry."

They arrived in the underground tunnels exactly on time. There was a slight buzzing sound and Commander Scarabee landed on Grayson's shoulder. "This," Grayson announced, "is Commander Scarabee."

The old beetle and the young boy stared at each other. "Is this for real?" Colin groaned. It was the beetle he had held captive a very long time ago; the very one he had failed to catch since then.

"Yes, it is very much *for real*," Grayson replied firmly. "You would be wise to remember that looks can be deceiving, particularly in the case of Commander Scarabee."

"But he couldn't even escape from a little rock fort," Colin muttered. "How can he possibly be of benefit on an important mission?"

The beetle glared at him but said nothing. Grayson, however, shook his head and turned his penetrating gaze to Colin. "Do you seriously believe he was caught?"

Colin looked at Grayson, doubt flitting across his face.

Grayson raised a brow at the boy. "You just saw for yourself that he can fly, so he could've just flown over the walls of your fort if he had truly wanted to escape."

Colin stared with new eyes at the beetle. Perhaps he had misjudged him, though he still could not see how such a little beetle could be of any help on such an important journey.

"Commander Scarabee has agreed to ride along on your hat. Heed any advice he gives you – he will not give any useless advice. Do I make myself clear?"

Colin straightened up and looked into Grayson's eyes. "Yes." He would show Grayson that he could be trusted. The message was concealed within his athame's sheath, and he would make sure it was delivered promptly and to the Abbot only, as Grayson had requested. And he would not linger but immediately return to Grayson's Mountain.

The warrior beetle landed lightly on the brim of Colin's hat. Grayson saluted him before placing his hand on Colin's shoulder. "It is a worthy journey you are taking. Good luck and Godspeed."

As he turned to go, he looked back. *Do not leave the path in front of you under any circumstance,* he reminded Colin sternly. As he strode off, he heard a squeaky voice shrill, "Let's get this show on the road." Grayson glanced over his shoulder as Colin rolled his eyes toward the brim of his hat, but started off, nonetheless. Grayson had attached a clear crystal to Colin's staff to light the way into the dark subterranean tunnel, though he still was not allowed to use the embedded crystals.

The passage was shadowy, but dry and cool. Not a sound broke the silence except for Colin's light footsteps on the stone floor. The beetle remained quiet, and for that Colin was thankful.

As he walked deeper into the tunnel, the quiet and the total aloneness began to seem less desirable and bordered on creepy instead. He could not see into the deepest shadows even when he shined the crystal towards them. He was a little appalled that the presence of the trickster warrior beetle began to bring him comfort. As he strode along humming softly to himself, he had no conception that his mission was anything other than the delivery of a message to a friend of Grayson's. He could not have imagined that it might help turn the tides of a great war that would engulf the whole of Terrene.

Grayson was even then hurrying into the Enchantment Room. He studied his crystal intently. Good. It hadn't changed. He stepped onto the balcony of his aerie and studied the land and the mountains before him. Quant had not returned. He would have to trust that he was okay. As he focused his mind on his old friend, a fleeting vision sped before his eyes. He saw Quant's fierce expression, his eyes glittering angrily, and heard his ferocious battle cry as he swooped downwards, his talons extended. It made Grayson's blood run cold.

His eyes closed for a moment. Then he was moving. In his chambers he threw on his cloak, strapped his sword, *bellum domitor,* over his back, and slammed his worn gray hat onto his head. He already wore his dagger, and his pentacle was always around his neck. He reached for his staff, mind racing. Things were moving faster than he had anticipated.

Striding towards the wood, he summoned Celeritas, the most noble and speediest of the mighty Friesian Wind-Walkers. He would need him on this journey.

As he hurried along the path, he attempted to order his mind. He couldn't dwell on those things he had already set in motion. Olcan. Phantom of the Sky. Colin and Commander Scarabee. Nor did he dwell on Quant, Lucas, or Aggie. They must now rely on their own strength, prowess, and innate knowledge. Along with a goodly supply of luck, he added wryly.

He turned his attention to Fingal's Land. The Defenders and all the people of this land would be instrumental in destroying Ben Toreke and his army of demons. The inhabitants of the other lands would be of significant assistance, also – the elves, fairies, and snow birds of the Land of Frozen Waters; the fierce dragons and giant birds of prey of the Northern and Derryveagh Mountains, giant wolves of the Cosmic Caverns Tundra, the creatures of the Kamahi, the gnomes of the Crystal Mountains and the Blue Forest, the Great Warrior Beetles of the Cagars, the fighting friars of the Forgotten Valley, the shy dragons of the Cagars, the Cefyll Dwr of the Blue River, and the Specter Cats of the Southern Plains. They were all old allies. But would they all stand together now? He would soon find out.

He was on his way to rally the mischievous beings of the Kamahi – the Isnana and the Piskies - and the gnomes of the Blue Forest. He shook his head and prayed they would cooperate without any of their usual shenanigans. He would bypass Fingal's Outpost. He hadn't the time for any interruptions and Murphy Byrne was a shrewd man; he would be in no need of guidance.

As he approached the small, lush meadow near the edge of the wood, Celeritas shook his great head, his wavy mane rippling in the slight breeze, and trotted to him. Grayson murmured his thanks to the mighty horse and swung onto his broad back, the horse's hooves already flying across the land by the time he had settled properly.

To get to the Blue Forest he must pass through the western-most edge of Fingal's Land. If there were people still in the tiny villages along his path, he would send them to Bodun. Alfred should be preparing his people to move to the eastern side of Fingal's River to form a massive line up to the Abhanmohr River to meet Hagan's troops from the north. If everything fell into place, the gnomes would join Alfred in defense of Fingal's southern half. The Kamahi inhabitants and the creatures of the Cosmic Caverns Tundra would join Hagan to defend the northern half.

The inhabitants of the Land of Frozen Waters would defend their southern border, and would also block access from the Gehenna into the Derryveagh Mountains. The fighting Friars of the Valley of the Forgotten Abbey were well equipped to savage the Gehenna occupants at the Valley's northern border. They also could attack from the Derryveaghs and the Misty Mountains.

Peter was even now sealing off his hidden lands and would join Colin and Commander Scarabee when they returned, along with the thousands of Warrior Beetles. They would defend the border between the Gehenna and the Southern Plains. Grayson could only imagine the shock Colin would feel when he returned to the Fearann Draiodh to face a war on Terrene the likes of which most of the inhabitants had never seen. The boy would have allies, so no harm would come to him. Grayson, of course, would see to it.

Grayson's eyes turned steely. He would have to destroy Ben Toreke. Again. This time he would have to destroy him so completely that there would be no way he could ever return.

As much as Grayson feared what he might see, he closed his eyes nonetheless, and summoned an image of Quant. He visualized him almost immediately, soaring through the fiery clouds, so high the tiny beings clustered below had no hope of catching him. As Grayson watched, Quant disappeared behind a dark cloud and was lost to sight. He blinked and broke into a smile. Quant had survived. Just as quickly, that same happy smile vanished, and he heaved a great sigh. Where were Lucas and Aggie?

Chapter Nineteen

Aggie and Lucas sat inside a cramped, filthy enclosure with barely enough room to sit and extend their legs out in front of them. It was suspended over the boiling lava inferno that was the Cauldron. The enclosure had two slits cut into the sides that allowed a modicum of the outside grayness to penetrate the blackness of the interior of their prison.

Aggie peered through one of the slits. She could glimpse the sky overhead and shuddered at the giant spider holes hanging low over the Cauldron. She was even more wary of them than usual because if the horrendously creepy, massive spiders that she imagined living there were to suddenly appear, she and Lucas would have no escape from the box they were imprisoned in.

Looking down was even worse. She could see the roiling lava underneath and the chaotic scene that was taking place on shore. The creatures below were vile and there was little to nothing human about them. Only the fact that they walked upright gave them a hint of an origin vaguely similar to her own. But they were ghastly with their misshapen, evil faces and their lurching gait. And there were so many of them! These monsters surely were not the Gehenna people?

As she watched, one of the creatures stepped away and turned his menacing eyes upwards. She moved quickly from the slit but not before his loud cackling told her he had seen her watching.

The enclosure suddenly plummeted downward, sending her sprawling. Lucas grabbed her and pulled her next to him. They held their breaths until the now familiar jolt brought their prison to a screeching halt – this time sending them both sprawling. Lucas clenched his teeth and made a low growling sound in his throat as the man below cackled even louder. How he would like to tear that freak limb from limb! If only there was a way to escape.

When they had come through the Sliabh Dearg, Aggie had found the secret door out of the mesa easily. They were unable to tell in the blackness of the tunnel whether it was dark enough outside to leave the safety of the mesa, but had calculated the time, drank a dose of invisibility potion, and slipped through the door.

All was quiet, and they had stayed in the shadow of the mesa as they ventured a little further afield. It was lighter than expected, though still gray, of course. Perhaps the slightly brighter light meant they were close to the fiery Cauldron.

As they rested for a moment, they had heard clanking sounds and voices that sounded far away. One could not always be sure how voices carried in different environments, so they would have to be careful. Keeping to any cover they could find, they sneaked closer. Even invisible, they would still hide if they could. No sense taking chances.

Their path led them to a camp of sorts. They slunk towards a narrow trench and lay down on their stomachs to watch. Lucas estimated there were at least a hundred people in the camp, if not more. Most were dressed in black robes with hoods that shadowed their faces. They made guttural sounds for the most part, but occasionally he heard a word or two he could understand. He looked at Aggie and she pointed towards the far right side of the camp.

Two of the creatures were beating someone with a club. The man they were beating was unlike them. He was also not like Aggie or Lucas. The glowing lava pools gave off just enough light for them to see that he was of slight build and dressed in light colored clothing. He made not a sound and it was all they could do not to go to his aid.

One of the black robed creatures finally gave him one last whack, motioned to his comrade, and retreated into the camp.

Aggie had been dismayed. Should they have attempted to help the person lying prone on the ground? After all, they were invisible. On the other hand, their ministrations to the wounded, or dead, man would be noticed. As she tried to decide, her breath caught, and she laid a hand gently on Lucas's arm. Two people, cowering low to the ground, had crept out of the shadows and were pulling the fallen man away. They were dressed as he was and even with light clothing were quickly swallowed up by the darkness.

Apparently, there were two factions at work here. Oppressors and oppressed? Who were they?

Aggie and Lucas slid backwards and headed away from the camp. They needed to find out how many of these black robed beings there were, for they were convinced that these were the adversaries they would have to defeat in order to save Terrene. Anything they could learn about them would be useful information to take to Hernsart.

Much later, after skirting two more camps, they topped a small rising and realized they had been on a higher elevation than they had thought. For far below them to the east lay the boiling lava lake known as the Cauldron. And surrounding it on all sides were hundreds of those same black robed creatures going about the business of preparing for war.

Stacks of weapons towered like small mountains around the northern perimeter of the Cauldron. Machines like nothing they had ever seen rumbled along, gobbling up the weapons with huge metal teeth. As they watched, shocked, more weapons were stacked, and several more machines pushed forward.

As they had stood, frozen at the sight, a tall figure a little removed from the main throng, turned towards them, his eyes staring straight at them. Aggie started, but Lucas held her arm. They were invisible and could only find each other by the string they had fastened around their wrists after the potion had taken effect. No way could someone find them from that distance. Quickly, though, they unfastened the strings and dropped them on the ground. Only then did they glance back toward the man, who had apparently sprouted wings, for he was in the air headed toward them. They dropped to the ground. There was no place to run. No place to hide. Aggie slowed her breath and kept her hand in Lucas's.

Then he was there. "I se-e-e-ee you!" he sang out, in an almost playful voice. They lay still until his foot nudged Lucas. Then they were on their feet, their swords drawn. The man was smiling as a net landed neatly over them. They attempted to cut the net with their swords, but the swords had just bounced off the nets, doing no damage at all.

The man called to them. "If you are through playing, we will get on with your interrogation. I assure you the nets will hold, so you are only wasting your energy."

"Who are you?" the man asked.

Aggie and Lucas remained silent, some part of them convinced that they could not be seen, not that they would have answered anyway.

"To what do I owe this untimely visit to my kingdom?" he boomed.

As they remained silent, he approached the net and landed a resounding kick on Lucas's wounded leg. Though it was all but healed, the pain was brutal, and he clenched his teeth to keep from screaming.

"Well, no matter," the man smirked. "You will talk soon enough. He threw back his hood revealing his skeletal, distorted features. What little skin he had was patchy and thin, his splintered bones protruding where no skin covered them; his eyes were hollow holes and his mouth looked painted on.

He laughed again as Aggie recoiled. What kind of creature was this that looked more like a dead man than anything alive, could fly, spoke their language, and apparently could see invisible beings?

"You will find it quite difficult to fight and win against dead men!" he exclaimed, as though he could read her thoughts. And with that, they had been hauled unceremoniously down to the Cauldron and with the jeers from their captors reverberating in their ears, were dumped, like fodder stored for animals, into the small enclosure they would come to loathe. Within minutes they found themselves suspended above the fiery lava lake.

Aggie was not given to self-pity, but now, as she and Lucas huddled in their miserable quarters above lava so hot it would cook them through before they touched the surface, she gave into it, wasted time though she knew it to be. They had felt the oppressive heat each time they were sent plummeting towards the Cauldron only to be pulled back up. It was a game to their captors, but they knew the vile leader's patience was wearing thin. The next time he might send them to their deaths; in fact, they weren't sure why he had kept them alive this long.

"We've got to get out of here," she whispered to Lucas, not for the first time. "It's only a matter of time before he tires of his game."

Lucas shook his head. They had discussed escape plans endlessly, but how exactly did one escape a prison high above a lake of boiling lava? He could kick the walls loose; they were made of wood so even his sore leg could possibly manage it. But what then? They couldn't see what they were hanging from so had no idea how to proceed.

Aggie had gone over and over in her mind the labels on the potion vials but could recall none that would help them in their present predicament. It was so dark in their prison they could only see vague images so she could not read the labels, plus they didn't want any of the creatures below to know that they had potions or the tiny lights that would shine like beacons if they were to be lit. She remembered that one of the tiny bottles had SS written on it, but did that mean shape shift? And if it did, what would they shapeshift into? A mouse might be helpful. They could scurry through the slits, across the top of the box and onto whatever held them up, and if they were very, very lucky might escape without plunging into the boiling lava below. But what if they changed into wolves, or dragons, or predator birds? Perhaps they would be able to fly away as a dragon or a bird before crashing into the lava, but they might end up worse off than they were now if they changed into creatures that could not fly. She snorted at the thought. *Could* they be any worse off?

She sighed, and Lucas put his arm around her. Tentatively, he asked, "Have you considered an attempt to communicate with Quant? He might still be in the area." He offered her a weak smile. "Though I daresay he might be so tired of rescuing us he'd be well within his rights to just leave us to our fate."

Aggie elbowed him in the ribs at his poor attempt at humor. "I do have to wonder how we have managed to get ourselves into so many sticky situations." She sighed again, "Maybe we're getting too old for all this."

"No," Lucas said. "We have done well. I know of no one who could've done better – human-wise, I mean." He sat up straight and turned Aggie's face toward his. "Try to contact Quant, or Grayson for that matter."

Aggie stared at him. The idea was preposterous. Sure, she could message Quant when he was right there before her, but she was nowhere near powerful enough to send messages across the entire countryside.

Lucas saw her look and said, "Don't dismiss the idea without some thought, Aggie. Our minutes are ticking away." He lifted her chin, "You have more power than you realize. I know it. And besides, what do you have to lose?"

Aggie bit her lip. Lucas was right. She knew Grayson's powers were extremely strong, so perhaps he would be able to hear her even back on Grayson's Mountain. And if Quant was still in the vicinity, he would surely hear her if she concentrated hard enough.

She nodded her head, "I will try. You're right. What do we have to lose?"

She moved away from Lucas and sat with crossed legs, her hands lying loosely on them, palms up. She closed her eyes, breathed deeply, and worked to clear all thoughts from her mind. She attempted to visualize Quant and after many minutes she was finally able to get a clear picture of him. He was at the top of a tall tree, his half-lidded eyes still.

She spoke with her mind. "Quant, if you can hear me, please come. Lucas and I are in a cage above the Cauldron with enemies all around us. We desperately need your help." She continued to visualize him and repeated her message. Finally, she opened her eyes and scooted over to nestle against Lucas's chest. He kissed her hair as they sat silently. Quant did not respond.

Outside, high above the Cauldron, Quant watched the box swinging gently above the sizzling, fiery waters. He had already been watching it for hours when he received Aggie's message. He could do little alone, but help was on the way. If only they could last that long. Not that he wouldn't attack alone if need be, but the outcome would be better with help. He closed one eye and dozed, the other watchful.

Aggie awoke to the usual cacophony of clanging, shouting, and loud machines. The hellish creatures were back at work preparing for war. A war that could devastate all that she held dear. If these vile, non-humans took over Terrene, there would be no Terrene left. And yet, here she sat, unable to warn those that could save her world.

Colin. Where was he? In Grayson's care he stood a chance of surviving. She sent a prayer up past the fiery clouds of the Gehenna to the heavens that he would be spared. That, somehow, Terrene would be spared. She thought of the fiery sky and the frightening spider holes above. Could a message to heaven even penetrate those hellish skies?

"So, humans, it is your day to die!" Their tormentor's voice boomed above the racket below. Aggie had named him "Bones", though that name was not nearly offensive enough for the likes of him.

"Unless, of course, you are ready to talk? If I were you, I would consider talking. Being boiled alive is not so much fun, I fear!"

They sat silently, Aggie's face buried in Lucas's shoulder.

"No?" came the taunting voice. "Don't worry. We make it fun." He cackled. "Not fun for you! But fun for me!"

Quant watched as the box fell ten feet and then caught. It was attached to a cable which was then fastened to a pulley. He could take out the ghoul operating the pulley, but what good would it do? Another one would just take his place and Quant would be dead. He needed a diversion at the right time and thought he knew what might work. As he watched, the box fell another ten feet. The leader chortled and jeered at the hapless occupants within. As the box fell, Quant felt, rather than heard, the vibration of giant wings closing in.

He screeched his most blood chilling shriek as he flew headlong toward the nearest machine, deadly talons extended, into the face of the machine operator. The operator lost control of the machine and veered into the weapons he had been collecting and through several more piles of weaponry before dropping with a clatter into the treacherous Cauldron.

Quant quickly regained speed and rushed at the horrible, shrieking creature who was in charge and screaming orders as he pointed a crossbow at Quant. Before he could release the arrow, however, Quant was on him, slashing and tearing at the madman's face. Then in a flash Quant zipped high into the air and into the fiery clouds, joining Sky Strike, who had managed to snap the cable that held Lucas's and Aggie's prison and now had the box with its precious cargo held tightly in his strong, massive talons. Aggie and Lucas were being jostled about mightily but were alive. And would soon be across the mesa and back to Fingal's Land.

Chapter Twenty

Colin and Commander Scarabee walked for miles through the narrow tunnel, the glow from the crystal lighting their way. Colin marveled at the tidy corridor. Nothing marred his path, and the walls were studded with glittering gems that sparkled when the light hit them. Deep inside the cavern the pathway widened and became more of a room than a tunnel.

Colin stopped and stared. There was a glowing bluish light shimmering off the walls and the ceiling of the room. He covered over his crystal and discovered that the surfaces continued to glow, casting ambient light throughout the room. He was amazed.

"Glowworms," Commander Scarabee announced in his squeaky voice. "Insect larvae," he added for good measure.

Colin stood transfixed. It was like some fairy world.

Commander Scarabee continued. "It's uncommon to see this bluish green color anywhere but in caves or deep in a shady forest. It's quite beautiful."

"It's like nothing I've ever seen," Colin whispered. "Maybe like thousands of fireflies all together. Except for the different color, of course."

Commander Scarabee didn't elaborate on the fact that he, himself, was bioluminescent under certain conditions. As were all the Great Horned Warrior Beetles. After a few moments he cleared his tiny throat and suggested they have a bite to eat while they enjoyed the shimmering cavern. Then they must be on their way.

Colin readily agreed. He was always hungry and dove into the pack Grayson had supplied. He hesitated as he looked through the tasty offerings, not knowing what Commander Scarabee might eat. There was cheese, bread, chicken, boiled eggs, dried figs, two pears, and celery. Plus two small round cakes. Colin's eyes lit up.

Commander Scarabee flew to the floor of the cavern and beckoned Colin away from the walls. "Let's sit out in the middle so we won't smush any of the larvae," he said, surveying the food as Colin laid out a small cloth and set out the food for their picnic.

Colin would just let the Commander choose what he wanted. As he reached for an egg, the Commander squeaked. "Would you be so kind as to pinch off a few pieces of one of those figs and a bit of celery?"

Colin obliged and placed the bits of food on one corner of the cloth. When they had eaten their fill, Colin re-packed the food that was left, folded the cloth and added it to the pack, strapped the pack on his back, and bade farewell to the glimmering glowworms.

Colin was sure that Grayson intended for them to move quickly towards the Abbey, so except for stopping to drink from one of the occasional small pools of crystal water, they walked on.

Finally, he grew so weary they had to stop. He was sure that Commander Scarabee was dozing up on his hat, judging from the soft buzzing sound he heard from time to time, but Colin had had no rest. He located a likely spot and laid down on the hard surface of the tunnel floor. They had not seen nor heard anything that would make them question their safety, and Colin went straight to sleep.

Hours later he awoke with no doubt at all that he had spent more hours than prudent stretched out on the cold, hard surface. But being young and resilient he stood, stretched, ate a crust of bread, and shared one of the pears with the Commander before they resumed their travel.

"We should reach the Abbey sometime this morning, I believe," Commander Scarabee mused, settling into his comfortable spot on the brim of Colin's hat.

The passageway grew narrow as they proceeded, so that if Commander Scarabee had not been a tiny bug, they would have had to resort to single file. It became colder and damper as they progressed. Water dripped from the ceiling and rivulets of water ran down the walls, apparently seeping out through the floor, as they saw no pools forming where the water ran.

Colin wondered at the narrowness of the corridor, finally saying to the Commander, "If this passageway continues to close in, you might have to go on alone!"

Which drew a squeaky "humph-h" from the Commander. "I daresay it must seem claustrophobic to you, but we must trust Grayson." He pondered a moment. "Though it leaves one to wonder what one might do if attacked."

Then added unnecessarily, "There is nowhere to hide and nowhere to run where one's back wouldn't be at a disadvantage."

These thoughts left Colin with all sorts of "what ifs" rumbling through his mind. But because they had been quite safe so far and there was nothing else to do, they plodded on, like lambs to slaughter.

The corridor twisted and turned all morning, leading ever skyward. Suddenly, stairs reached upwards to a gorgeous, magical looking door. It was gracefully arched and looked to be a painting of trees against a moonlit sky. Colin stopped short, almost casting the Commander off his perch. "Wow," Colin said reverently, advancing slowly. He reached out his hand to touch it and was amazed when his hand disappeared. He jerked it back. This was no door! He wondered briefly if it might be a portal but dismissed that idea as preposterous.

"Hold onto y . . ., *my* hat, Commander, we're going through," he said, plunging forward.

On the other side he was not surprised to see that the "door" had disappeared. It was as though he and the Commander had passed through the solid wall of the mountain. How in the world would he find his way back?

He had no time to study the area and get his bearings, however, as a young man not much older than him was heading up a path directly towards them. He had dark features and wore loose pants and a long tunic split on both sides, both of which were as red as the roses that ambled along the garden wall back on Grayson's Mountain. The man's feet were covered in soft flat shoes. His face was composed, and he bowed his head briefly as he reached Colin.

Colin introduced himself, and seeing that the man was eyeing Commander Scarabee with some alarm, introduced him as well, feeling somewhat foolish. "I have a message for Abbot Tomas Fergus Galloway," he said in his best imitation of Grayson. The man did not speak, but pointed down the path from whence he came, motioning Colin to go first.

Colin was at a loss. First of all, he had never seen scarlet clothes and thought it odd for a monk to wear pants, let alone red ones. Shouldn't they be wearing robes? Secondly, he wasn't particularly happy for the unknown man to be behind him rather than in front. Also, there was a pervasive silence about the man that surely could not be natural.

As Colin descended the forest path, he began to notice sounds other than those normally associated with a forest. He could see what looked like a wide, open space ahead where the trees stopped short, and when he approached the precipice was amazed at the sight of a vast rooftop below that seemed to go on forever. The rooftop was flat and walled, with several towers around the perimeter, and one ornate, massive tower protruding from the center of the rooftop. The large tower had a portico surrounding it with colossal columns that reached to the rooftop of the structure. Interspersed between the columns were magnificent arched windows and doors. A huge stone cross was mounted high atop this middle tower.

Even more astonishing than the magnificent architecture of the building was the sight of a multitude of scarlet clothed monks with long sticks, similar to Colin's staff, involved in some sort of intricate movements, dancelike, yet warlike as well. They moved as one, leaping and swaying gracefully, yet brandishing their sticks aggressively.

As Colin watched, spellbound, he began to recognize some of the movements – the same movements he and Grayson used when fighting with their staffs. Fighting monks? Who had ever heard of such a thing?

The man led them to an inconspicuous gate a few feet through the forest to their left. The gate opened at his touch onto a tiny landing which gave way to narrow stairs going down to the roof. Colin wasn't surprised to find that the stairs and the gate faded from sight as they accessed the roof.

The middle tower was apparently their destination for the man led them on a straight path directly to it. Once there, they entered through an arched doorway, and entered a magnificent open room. Colin gawped at the glorious room before remembering Grayson's admonishments and snapped his mouth shut. The man realized he had lost his followers and turned around. Noticing Colin's astonishment as he surveyed the room, he stood silently and allowed him to inspect the tower.

The room was circled by tall open arches. Two of the arches were doorways and the rest were windows. These windows were built up from the floor about as high as a comfortable seat, and decorative pillars reached about two thirds of the way to the peak of the arch. Carvings of men and landscapes ran from the top of the pillars to the apex of the arch. Two of the window seats were not seats at all Colin discovered as he wandered further into the large room. They held a rocky soil, with lighted candles pushed down into the sand. The flickering lights were beautiful in the daylight; Colin could only imagine how peaceful they would be at night. Stars and candlelight were beacons in the dark, and he admired them both.

The ceiling was arched across the room and made of unevenly patterned stones of dark gray that obviously had been around for more years than seemed possible. The floor was clay colored and gray with no discernable pattern to the layout. Colin thought it quite attractive. Perfectly round windows set above the arches let even more light in, and he again marveled at the superb and harmonious architecture. He was certainly no expert, but it all went together quite well in his humble opinion.

He was feeling a bit dazed by the cathedral-like splendor of the room when he belatedly noticed the silent man waiting for them and hastened to join him. Quickly reaching a wide staircase lighted by torches, they walked down the stairs and entered a wide torchlit corridor. The only sound was the light tapping of his shoes – the silent man's shoes making no sound at all - as they walked. A minute or two of walking and the darkness of the corridor became lighter. Colin was amazed to see a beautiful courtyard to his left. He couldn't stop himself from staring. It was so large it seemed endless. Rows of fruit trees, berry bushes, and row upon row of possibly every known edible plant in Terrene formed a massive, well-tended garden. Stone pathways led through the rows, and he could hear water burbling, though it was not visible.

He realized he had stopped, absorbed in the enchantment of it all. Reluctantly he pulled his eyes from the garden and found the man again patiently waiting. As soon as he locked eyes with Colin, he started down the corridor again, Colin trailing behind, still glancing at the garden as he walked along, until the corridor closed in again and the peaceful sight was hidden behind the stone walls.

In just a few minutes, he was led into a small room with nothing in it but two benches facing each other, and a large, decorative, closed wooden door with a large cross carved into it at the far end. It was eerily quiet. No one seemed to be about. Maybe the inhabitants of the place were all above on the roof. He shook his head at all the dazzling sights he had been fortunate enough to see in just the past hour.

The man motioned for him to sit, and then entered the closed door. Colin peered into the corridor, which continued past where they sat. He could see huge arched doorways leading off in all directions - to the many areas inside the monastery, Colin supposed. If the rooftop was any indication of the size of the building, he guessed the monks were worn out by the end of the day after traversing an area so large. The roof itself seemed to reach to the surrounding mountains on all sides, covering the entire valley floor except for the garden area. Colin had seen sunshine spilling over the plants so that area must be open to the sky. That made sense since he knew no other way plants could survive. But where were their animals? Surely, they had an abundance of those. He sighed. He would love to be allowed to roam freely throughout this intriguing place.

Commander Scarabee had been so quiet, Colin wondered if he were still in residence upon his hat. "Commander," he whispered, "are you still there?"

"Of course I'm still here!" the Commander squeaked more loudly than Colin thought prudent. "Where else would I be?"

"Shh-h-h," Colin placed his finger across his lips. "I don't think we're supposed to talk in here," he whispered.

He heard a rustle nearby and jumped. The man had appeared on silent feet and motioned him to follow. He was led through the door the man had entered earlier and found a dapper, pink-faced, wrinkled man only a head taller than Colin himself. He was wearing a white robe with a red sash and greeted Colin cheerfully. "I am Abbot Tomas," he said. "Who might you be?"

He seemed friendly enough, but his eyes bore into Colin's. He was apparently a man who brooked no nonsense, so Colin got right to the point. "I am Colin Ceartas, a messenger from Grayson Ghlic. Perhaps you know him?" he asked hesitantly.

The Abbot perked up at the mention of Grayson's name and motioned at the silent man who had been standing – guarding? – the door that he could leave them, which he did, closing the door firmly behind him.

As the Abbot sank into the chair behind a broad table stacked with books and papers, he motioned for Colin to sit opposite him. Colin noticed that the room was much larger than he had thought. It had an arch that connected it to a bright room with a comfortable seating arrangement and a table with four chairs. Another door led off of it.

Abbot Tomas peered closely at Colin's hat. "Commander, is that you?"

"Ahem," the Commander coughed. "Yes, it is, Your Excellency."

The Abbot protested the title, "Call me Abbot Tomas, please. Both of you. We don't stand on formality much around the monastery." Settling into his chair more comfortably, he said, "Welcome, Commander. It's been a long time."

"Indeed, it has," the Commander sighed, remembering those long-ago times.

"You must be famished. Let us have a spot of refreshment while we talk." He tinkled a tiny bell and the silent man reappeared.

This was getting almost humorous, Colin thought, as the man received his orders from the Abbot and retreated.

Returning to Colin's question at last, the Abbot replied, "To answer your question, young man, I do indeed know Grayson Ghlic, as you call him."

When Colin didn't respond, the Abbot prodded him, "Come then, you have a message for me?"

Colin tucked away the thought that was gnawing at him: the Abbot had said, "as you call him". What did that mean? Suddenly he realized the Abbot was waiting on him and he stood with a start, jerking his athame from its sheath. He gasped as a sword point materialized at his throat. The silent man held a tray of refreshments in one hand and a sword in the other and had thrust himself between Colin and the Abbot.

There was a sound like rumbling thunder, and a blinding light, followed by Colin being shoved backwards as a colossal Commander Scarabee sprang between a prostrate Colin and the threatening sword. "Stop immediately," he said, his voice no longer the least bit squeaky, but bold and commanding. The sword never wobbled, but didn't slice his throat either. That had to be promising.

"The boy's note is in his knife sheath. He was not attacking anyone, though his movements were certainly those of a flighty boy rather than the powerful wizard that he is." He looked piercingly at Colin.

Colin cringed at being called flighty but puffed up a bit at the powerful wizard part. He slowly stood, his mind a whirl of spells that might be at his disposal if things got more out of hand.

"Colin," Commander Scarabee ordered in a no-nonsense voice, "Pull the note from your sheath and replace the knife immediately!"

Colin scrambled to do as he was told. He handed the note carefully to the Commander, who in turn handed it to the Abbot across the table. "For God's sake, man, get that infernal sword out of my face," he demanded of the abbot's assistant. His beetle brows were bunched in irritation.

The Abbot skimmed the note before looking up and motioning the man to remove his sword - which he did, though not without a slight scowl before his impassive face returned. He continued to hold his sword in one hand as he gracefully set the refreshment tray on the tabletop near the Abbot with the other.

The Abbot signaled with his eyes that the silent man was free to go before reclaiming his chair and motioning the Commander and Colin to sit down. He stared at the Commander. "I like you in your present form best, Commander." He raised his eyebrows at Colin. "He is quite impressing, don't you agree?"

Colin glanced at the Commander, who in truth was quite frightening, and nodded before the Abbot spoke again in firm, measured tones. "It was a dangerous and stupid thing you did in drawing your knife so threateningly. You could have been killed. Some would not stop at a sword to the throat but would have sliced your head clean off your neck."

Colin blanched and thought he would be sick. He swallowed hard and finally found his voice. "You are right, Abbot Tomas. I presumed a great many things and forgot that we are strangers to you and so not trustworthy until proven so. I apologize most humbly,"

The Commander looked on him with new eyes. "Bravo, lad!" he couldn't help roaring.

The Abbot spoke. "*You* are a stranger, it's true. But I have known Commander Scarabee long years and trust him completely." The Commander nodded at the Abbot. "However, my assistant knows neither of you and would naturally be protective. You might bear your actions in mind and work hard to improve them so that an episode such as we've just witnessed will not happen again."

Colin, his face pink with embarrassment, felt justly chastised and thanked the Abbot for his advice. The Abbot poured the tea and slid cups toward them both before pouring his own and taking a sip. "If you'll excuse me, I will read Grayson's missivmore thoroughly." He pushed the plate of delectable looking cakes toward them and flipped open the note.

When he completed his reading, taking sips of the tea as he read, he stood. "It seems there is a bit of urgency, and I must hasten to follow Master Grayson's instructions. We have much to do, it seems, and very little time. Enjoy your repast, and my assistant will show you the way out when you are ready. Please take your time."

The Commander stood and smiled a smile that on him looked more like a fierce grimace. "Thank you for your hospitality, Abbot. We will be on our way. Grayson bade us not to linger, so we must get back. If you would be so kind as to summon your man, we will be on our way." He followed the Abbot into the anteroom, Colin bringing up the rear, still holding one of the half-eaten cakes. "Have you a message for Grayson?" the Commander asked as he noticed the silent man already waiting in the corridor.

The Abbot nodded, his eyes locked with those of the Commander, "Tell him that he can count on us. Now I must bid you Godspeed. I hope that we may meet again under more pleasant circumstances."

Turning to Colin, he nodded briefly. "Take care, young wizard," he advised, before hurrying away in the opposite direction to which the silent man now motioned Colin and the Commander.

Colin swallowed the rest of the cake in one huge bite as he sped along the corridor with the Commander and the silent man. A muffled gong sounded three times from the depths of the Abbey.

Chapter Twenty-One

Grayson swung from the broad back of his mighty horse and stared at the yawning opening in the rock wall of the mountain. He could've ridden Celeritas right into the massive hole, but knew that all horses, including the mightiest and the calmest, are repelled by underground structures. He couldn't say he blamed them when the structures were as dank as many subterranean habitats were. The gnomes of the Blue Forest had never been known for beauty of any kind, except perhaps for the glittering gems and gold they hoarded away in the darkness of the gloomy caverns. Some said the gems were so luminous they lit up entire areas of the inside of the mountain.

Grayson laid a hand on Celeritas and surveyed the area more closely. Large trees near the opening to the mountain had been cut and the pieces thrown helter-skelter into two towering piles. It was eerily quiet.

"Tabhair aire do sheaschara," he whispered. *Take care old friend.*

He headed towards the opening, taking one last look around outside before cautiously entering the gray gloom of the interior. He had hoped to encounter one of the gnomes close to the entrance, but apparently he was not to be that lucky today.

Gnomes could disappear straight down into the earth itself if threatened, so he would have to proceed carefully. He needed to talk to them, and even a wizard could not survive where there was no air to breathe.

He followed the sounds of garbled voices to a large room with a fire blazing in the middle, making it less bleak. The logs crackled and sizzled as the gnomes worked busily in the hazy, smoky room. There was a slight updraft of smoke, so there had to be some sort of ventilation – enough to keep one from asphyxiation, but not nearly enough to clear the room of smoke. Perhaps if they could breathe under the ground, smoke didn't bother them.

He watched from outside the room for a moment, hidden in the shadows, before stepping forward and hailing the little people. The gnomes looked startled, but before they could fade away, a raspy voice hailed him. "Hello, Wizard," the leader of the gnomes said from his small perch at the side of the room.

Grayson smiled and hurried forward. "Hello, Poppo. It's been a long time."

The little man looked at him cannily and grinned, his entire face wrinkling up. "And sorry it is not longer." He looked pointedly at Grayson, and Grayson nodded his head. "You must have bad news, wizard, or perhaps you are lost?" Poppo asked with a smirk.

Grayson coughed and glanced around at their audience. He did not wish to discuss his business with all the gnomes. He would leave that for Poppo to do after he had taken his leave.

Poppo recognized the glance for what it was and pushed himself up, barking for the other gnomes to get back to their own business. Grayson followed the retreating back of the diminutive gnome into the corridor. After a couple of turns, they entered a room that dazzled with crystals.

Grayson glanced around the room. "Your crystals are flawless, as always," he complimented the gnome. "I will be in the market for some more after all this . . ." he stopped, and with a sigh, sank down onto a large stone. "Well, we'll just have to see what happens." The wrinkled, white-haired gnome watched him and said nothing.

"You are right that I bring bad news. To get right to it, the Gehenna has been invaded by Death Reapers." He hesitated before finishing his statement. "Led by Ben Toreke, I'm afraid."

Poppo did not react except for a quick intake of breath. "I'm sure I don't know how he could have returned when he was as dead as anyone could be, and burned to a crisp at that," he spat. Gnomes had as much reason as anyone to hate Ben Toreke. Many of their number had been killed and their treasures stolen by the man.

Grayson glanced down at his hands which lay folded in his lap before meeting the gnome's eyes and saying quietly, "Terrene is threatened with destruction. War is coming. And soon."

Poppo's eyes widened.

"No one is safe," Grayson proclaimed. "Ben Toreke has escaped from Hell with thousands of Death Reapers. He is preparing for war on Terrene. *All* of Terrene! That includes the gnomes," he stressed. "I have little time to convince you, but know that it is true. You must bolster your caves and make them impenetrable. Hide your treasures."

Softening his tone, Grayson reminded the leader of the gnomes, "You have fought before, and the gnomes' cunning and expertise with the hammer and axe are legend." He looked shrewdly at Poppo, pursing his lips, his eyes twinkling. "And potions, I might add."

Poppo drew himself to his full height of two feet, one inch. The wizard had never lied to the gnomes. Poppo was old and did not relish war, but he would defend his home.

Grayson watched intently as Poppo's mind worked to sort through the things required of him. "We will secure the mountain – and the treasures. Then we will travel underground to the Misty Mountains prepared to do our part."

Grayson stood. "Fair enough." He stared into space before saying quietly, "None of us wants this war, but we must defend ourselves, our friends, and our homes."

Poppo grunted. "Will you eat before you go?"

Grayson shook his head. "Thanks, but I must go. Another time perhaps."

Grayson and Celeritas were crossing over the Blue River by noon and approached the border of the Kamahi Forest before nightfall. Celeritas moved quickly, sometimes speeding across the ground like a gusty wind; sometimes his feet leaving the ground completely as he soared just above the surface. Grayson set up camp underneath one of the gnarled, twisted Kamahi trees that formed the border between the Blue Forest and the Kamahi Forest.

The trees within the Kamahi Forest are covered with moss, lichens, ferns, and hanging vines. The Isnana, large brown venomous spiders, live in burrows beneath the tangle of vines and briar patches near the River of Death. If he was lucky, Grayson would be able to avoid them. He would stay within the eastern part of the forest and hope they were keeping to their usual territory to the west. He had no intention of straying from the path that led to the piskies' encampment. And to be even more safety minded, he would travel only by day into this forbidding land. Hence his decision to camp beneath the ancient kamahi tree. Even a wizard had his limits, and the Isnana were his. Not that he couldn't best them if push came to shove, but they were so repulsive and relentless he would prefer to leave it to the piskies to handle them.

The day dawned with dancing sunbeams penetrating the heavy foliage, brightening both the day and Grayson's spirits. The threat of war loomed heavily over him, but, nevertheless, he felt buoyed by the knowledge that Terrene's people and creatures were stalwart and smart. They would fight aggressively, each group using their special powers to destroy the intruders that threatened them.

He and Celeritas plodded along enjoying the occasional sun shaft warm on their shoulders as the canopy above opened up and spilled the sunlight onto the forest floor. The vegetation was over-grown and rubbed Celeritas' belly in a few places as he walked along. Even so, the path was well-trodden and visible enough for the most part to follow easily, and they made good time. At one point, late in the morning, Celeritas hesitated at a sort of crossroads and waited for Grayson to point the way.

Grayson had no memory of a crossroads and was puzzled. The piskies' settlement should be straight ahead, but what of this other path that intersected? He was studying each of the paths and had decided that the way was straight ahead when he heard a noise like buzzing bees. He looked to his right to see two piskies sauntering down the path towards him, chattering like magpies.

"Hello," he startled them. They had been so lost in their prattle they jumped and then tittered before moving a few steps closer. They looked at the tall man on the gigantic horse suspiciously but were too curious to run away.

As they stared, Grayson called to them, "I am looking for Darius. Could you by chance direct me to his abode?"

The piskies exchanged looks. What in the world was an abode? They tittered again in their confusion. They both had flaming hair and were wrinkled like little old men. Their hands flapped in the air as they jabbered to each other like crows, glancing at Grayson from time to time. They were dressed in ragged moss-colored clothing that blended into the forest, though their hair was too flamboyant to easily hide. The grass along the path came to their waists, but they seemed to have no trouble plowing along through it. It would provide excellent cover if they decided to disappear.

Grayson watched them as they talked. "It's a simple question," he finally offered. "Do you know Darius, and if so, do you know where he lives?"

The chattering piskies stopped, exchanging a look before one of them pointed his long finger down the road in front of him. "That would be the way," he said. "You've still a far distance to go, so best be getting on."

Grayson peered down the path to his left. That would've been the last path he would've chosen. Piskies were known for their pranks, and he was convinced these two were up to no good. Nonetheless, he pretended to turn Celeritas in that direction. After only a few steps, he looked over his shoulder at the piskies, who had not moved.

"Thank you very much. I'm sure Darius will appreciate your helping me. He is a great friend of mine." He looked shrewdly at the two piskies as he reached into a bag hanging on his saddle and brought out two piskie-sized moss green coats and two pairs of soft leather shoes. "As soon as I find Darius I will apprise him of your assistance, and you may claim these clothes as a reward."

The piskies stared at the clothes as they disappeared back into Grayson's bag. The one who had not pointed the direction to Grayson stepped smartly ahead of his friend, "Allow me to introduce myself," he said grandly. "My name is Spriggan and I'm afraid my friend inadvertently misinformed you," he croaked. "He's always getting lost and really can't find his way to his own house most of the time." For good measure he glared at his friend before returning his gaze to Grayson. "You would be much wiser to follow the path you were on. I'm sure King Darius will be happy to see you, Sire. Just tell him Spriggan and Mosey were the ones who helped you find your way."

Grayson nodded noncommittally, thanked the two pranksters, and turned back onto the path he had originally been on. He realized they had tried to send him straight to the River of Death and into Isnana territory. If they truly wished him harm that would've elevated a mere prank to a much more sinister consequence. With piskies, one never knew, but he would alert Darius, just in case.

Shadows were beginning to overtake the land when Celeritas topped a hillside overlooking the ancient stone circle and the underground barrows that housed the ancient kin of the piskies. It was a beautiful sight. The gnarled trees and heavy growth did not impinge on the open area surrounding the ancient standing stones, and enough sunlight still pierced the canopy to dapple the stones with fading light. The piskies made their homes underground near the graves of their forebears.

Twilight was falling, which heralded the time of feasting and dancing. The piskies would be gathering soon, and Darius would preside.

Celeritas picked his way down the hillside and stopped at one of the standing stones where Grayson dismounted. "The grass looks quite good here in the open. Eat your fill and rest." Grayson knew the piskies loved horses so didn't think they would be up to any tricks where Celeritas was concerned. He was a canny horse, anyway, and would be wary of their tricks. He could more than take care of himself.

Grayson sat down on a large flat boulder to await the arrival of the journeying piskies he had met along the way. He assumed they were coming this way but could not be positive. He sighed and lit his pipe. He had little time to waste, but would have to woo Darius carefully.

Darius was the most somber of the unruly piskies, albeit he was still a piskie, with piskie ways. Perhaps Grayson could approach the coming war as a huge prank! The piskies would certainly want a hand in what they would undoubtedly consider a truly magnificent escapade. He considered the idea for a moment but knew he must present the facts as he knew them and let the cards fall where they might. He would not ensnare even piskies in a war that might decimate all of Terrene. They would have to join willingly.

The buzzing of Spriggan and Mosey broke the silence as they skipped into the clearing. Grayson wondered if they were ever quiet. Not likely. At almost the same instant, other piskies appeared from all around the circle, stopping short as Grayson stood and put his pipe away. He glanced at Celeritas, who continued to chomp the succulent grasses completely unperturbed, the stamp of a hoof the only move he made to acknowledge that he knew the piskies had appeared. It was a warning to them of the power of those massive hooves.

The piskies stared from Grayson to the horse, not quite knowing how to proceed with a stranger in their midst. Suddenly, Darius swept into the clearing, announcing in a jolly voice, "Let the festivities begin!" He clapped his hands and looked around. Spying Grayson, he added, "Come, come. We have an important guest to entertain. Bring out our best food and plenty of ale."

As the piskies scurried to do his bidding, Darius made his way over to Grayson, motioning him back to the stone he had been sitting on. The diminutive king was less than two feet tall and nearly as round as he was tall. He was hideous in looks, but dressed in finery befitting a king, tattered though it was. He had a regal bearing and was proud of his station among the piskies.

Several of the piskies rushed to bring in a throne of sorts so that their king would be on the same level as the tall intruder. Darius climbed upon it and sank wearily into the cushions. They also set up a table between the two, strewing colorful flowers and mosses across the top.

Grayson and Darius talked in generalizations as the piskies prepared the feast. They were each then served from heavy trays laden with food carried by two brawny piskies. Piskie-sized loaves of coarse bread were added to the table, along with tankards of ale.

Grayson could only imagine how he must look with his piskie-sized tankard held between two fingers, and his knees protruding up beside the small table. The food was plentiful, however, and there was a hefty pitcher of ale plunked onto the table as well.

It was against the rules of piskie etiquette to discuss business while eating, so he bided his time, enjoying the tender morsels of meat of unknown origin – some kind of bird he imagined - along with cracked nuts, savory shoots of vegetation, crisp apples, and moist honey cakes. The bread was heavily grained and chewy, and the ale was fruitier than he was used to, but delicious. He complimented Darius on the meal before deftly beginning to maneuver the conversation around to the reason for his visit. First, though, he broached the subject of his conversation with Spriggan and Mosey on the road.

At the mention of the miscreants' names, Darius stopped a chunk of bread an inch from his mouth and stared at Grayson, trying to gauge the outcome of the encounter. Grayson's lips twitched upwards a fraction which might be a good sign the king decided, as he stuffed the bread into his mouth.

"They were quite helpful – after a fashion," Grayson related, careful not to imply that the piskies had purposely attempted to send him to what they would've considered his doom. He was, after all, a wizard, and a wise one it was told. He had realized they were steering him wrong, but another traveler might not be so perceptive. Perhaps he should've followed his first inclination when he had the chance and turned them into wild sorrel – a plant highly prized and eaten as a delicacy by piskies. It would've served them right to be devoured by their own brethren. He had to hold back a chuckle at the thought.

"I'm sure they were," Darius said with a fair amount of doubt. "With those two about it's a wonder you are here to tell the tale."

Grayson waved his concern away. "Well, all's well that ends well," he said, chewing a morsel of honey cake before adding, "they bear watching, however."

Darius chortled, "An understatement if I've heard one." He downed his second tankard of ale and nodded. "I'm all too aware of their misdeeds. They decided one night to start the bonfire for the feast and dropped a bowl of nut shells in the fire." His face darkened. "You should have seen them when the nuts began to explode! They could've burned the entire forest down." He shook his head in despair. "And that's just one example. Haven't got a brain between them, so I doubt they've learned their lesson."

"Probably not," Grayson agreed. "I regret now that I promised them coats and shoes for their help. Thought it might help them learn that good deeds are rewarded."

"Humph-h-h!" snorted the piskie king. "You better hand over those outfits to me so I can attach severe consequences to them. Otherwise, you've wasted your time – and good clothing in the bargain!"

When the feasting was over and the music in full swing, Grayson and Darius removed themselves from the circle and into the shadowy night. They stopped near where Celeritas stood quietly, having filled his belly with the tasty grass. Stars were twinkling above them, and the moon was just beginning to rise. Grayson sat on a log so he wouldn't tower over the small piskie king.

"What brings you to the Kamahi?" Darius asked. "I'm pretty sure it's not a social call." He watched the piskies frolicking about and playing tricks on their fellow piskies when the opportunity arose. He was a skillful ruler and managed his flock of unruly piskies competently and with as much humor as he could muster, but he had to practice patience, for he had little time for the pranks and mischief most of his underlings were so keen on. Without looking at Grayson, he said, "Perhaps it has something to do with the strange goings-on in Gehenna land?"

The question took Grayson by surprise, though he should've realized that Darius was shrewd and curious about the other beings in Terrene. Especially the elves. Simon would've talked to the elves by now, so they would know what was coming. It would be normal to pass that information on. And Grayson realized that Darius was astute enough to have his spies scattered about where it mattered.

Grayson glanced around. This world, even with piskie pranks, giant spiders, and so many other species living on the land, was a beautiful place, a place well worth protecting. He looked knowingly at Darius.

"What have you been told?"

"War is surely coming," said the diminutive king. He blew out a breath. "We will help where we can."

"Thank you," Grayson said. "I fear that if we don't all do our best to quell the marauders we will all pay a huge price." With a serious expression, he added, "Ben Toreke has escaped from Hell's Door with thousands of Death Reapers." He gazed at the standing stones, the flowery meadow nearby, the tiny waterfall cascading from the far hill. This was only one tiny part of a beautiful and mostly harmonious world. It was a shame all creatures could not live peacefully among their fellow beings. He sighed. "We must all do our best," he repeated, this time more passionately.

Darius merely nodded. He had learned of Ben Toreke's escape already and would do his part to save Terrene.

"Here is what I'd like the piskies to do," Grayson said. He looked around to make sure none of the curious piskies had wandered closer. When he saw none, he bent low and whispered his request into Darius's pointy ear.

The piskie king looked startled at Grayson's request, then laughed so hard he was struck by a coughing fit, which he overcame only after a couple of raps on his back from Grayson.

Once the king had settled down, Grayson reached into his bag and handed him the piskie outfits to do with what he thought best. He then shook the king's tiny hand, mounted Celeritas, and saluted Darius. "Beimid ag troid go dti an deireadh." *We will fight to the end.*

He had no qualms about riding at night if no mammoth, deadly spiders, or pesky piskies were about. Besides, the festivities had gone on for so long it was almost dawn. He and Celeritas faded into the trees and were soon swallowed by the darkness.

Chapter Twenty-Two

Peter was waiting for Colin and Commander Scarabee when they entered the lodge of Fearann Draoidh. He had transformed from a quiet farmer and shepherd to a presence more befitting the powerful general that he was in his tall, polished boots, peaked cap, and gleaming medals.

Colin stared at him, stunned, as Commander Scarabee, who had traveled back from the Forgotten Abbey as a small beetle atop Colin's hat, suddenly evolved into his frightening, monstrous other self and greeted *General* McEvoy.

Peter smiled at Colin, greeting him and the Commander, before handing him a sealed note. Colin looked from one to the other, but as there was nothing forthcoming from either, he broke the seal, which he recognized as belonging to Grayson, and skimmed the note.

Predictably, it was written in Grayson's flowing, bold handwriting.

Colin, it began, *there is no easy way to prepare you for what has transpired, so I will not mince words. Terrene is preparing for war.* Startled, Colin glanced up to see two pairs of interested eyes watching him intently. He turned his back and continued reading. *I will be at Hagan's fortress when you read this. You must go immediately to the Enchantment Room. When you enter, speak my name into the reflecting stone and I will explain what you must do. General McEvoy and Commander Scarabee should remain within the lodge itself while you are doing this. They are to be trusted completely, but wizard business belongs only to wizards. Offer them what refreshments you have at hand. When it is time for them to go, I will whisk them out. Leave that to me. Hurry.*

It was unsigned.

When Colin had hastily read the note a second time, he stuffed it into his pocket and promptly led the imposing general and the massive insect to the table where he and Grayson took their meals. "I must attend to a task," he said, as he placed a wedge of hard cheese, a chunk of bread, and water in front of them. "I won't be long," he announced as he sped off.

Peter called, "Take your time and give Grayson our greetings. Tell him we await his command."

Colin faltered a step but did not stop as he realized Peter must know what his mission was.

Peter smiled at the Commander as he broke the bread in two.

"You know?" the Commander asked quietly.

Peter shook his head. "Only that the note is from Grayson. I have no idea what the boy's task is, but presume Grayson will deliver it directly to him." He swallowed a chunk of bread and downed the cup of water. "We will be involved in whatever it is, or else we wouldn't be here."

The Commander nodded, his antennae at attention and his beetle brows furrowed in thought.

Colin thought Grayson looked somewhat more haggard than usual as he appeared in the reflecting stone. He was, however, dressed in garb more befitting a wizard than his usual clothes - a faded midnight blue, hooded robe with some of nature's most powerful symbols etched into the cuffs and along the hem – stars, the moon, a cross, sun, lightning. A fearsome dragon, barely visible, coiled around the band of his wide brimmed, slightly conical hat. He held his staff, and his magnificent sword, *bellum domitor*, was strapped at his hip. Colin was sure his dagger was close at hand and that his pentagram lay hidden beneath his cloak. Grayson had been transformed from resembling a mere mortal man into a powerful immortal wizard. Colin stood transfixed as he took it all in.

Grayson chuckled. "You will find a new cloak of your own on your clothes peg. It has powers of its own which will magnify your own powers." He wiped the smile from his face and said, "Now you must listen carefully. We have little time. First, let me assure you that your parents are alive and in good health, and Quant is here with me." Grayson held his hand up to stop the torrent of questions he knew Colin had. "We have no time. You, Peter, and the Commander must begin preparations. War has come to Terrene."

Colin took a breath and blew it out, straightened up, and nodded.

"Good. Commander Scarabee must prepare his troops. He will know what to do. Tell him to take them through the Sky Tube and disembark at the exit east of Trenton in two days' time. They will await further instructions there. If they are attacked at any time, they are to pummel the enemy with all the power at their disposal.

Peter will have his wind-walkers ready, and they, too, need to protect the borders of the Great Southern Plains. Tell him to summon the Specter Cats, the black panthers of the Plains. The panthers and the dragons of the Cagars will protect the area near you – the Fearann Draiodh, the wood, and the Cagars." Grayson searched Colin's face. He was relieved and gratified to see only determination and grit written there.

"You will have the power, with your new cloak, to summon energy you don't realize you have. Wear your armor underneath your cloak, and be sure you are dressed for battle, just in case. You are stronger than you know. You must believe in yourself and do your best." He smiled a small smile at Colin. "You must protect all of the land within sight of the Fearann Draiodh. Help Peter and his wind-walkers and their neeston riders, Commander Scarabee's troops, and the Specters. Be an added pair of eyes, ears, and hands. Use your power – all of it – as needed. The dragons, by the way, can take care of themselves."

He paused as he continued to look at Colin. "Go and rest for a while, for when the battle begins, you will have no time for such luxuries. Have food prepared that you can grab on the run. In two days' time you must go to the Enchantment Room and remain there or on the balcony. I will communicate through the reflecting stone, and you can visualize any area of the Plains, the woods, and the Cagars, in the cauldron. Godspeed."

As Grayson began to fade, Colin shook his head. "No. No! Wait!" But Grayson merely said, "We must all protect Terrene to the best of our abilities. You are powerful, and quite capable. Don't doubt it." And he was gone.

Colin tried with all his might to summon him back, but to no avail. He had a million questions – about his parents, the war, his duties, the enemy. Who were they? And dragons? He tried to shake loose any memory he had of dragons in the Cagars. Except for Phantom of the Sky he had no memory of ever knowing that other dragons existed. He had no way of knowing that all of Terrene was dragon land.

He hunched his shoulders as he left the Enchantment Room. On his own he feared he didn't have enough knowledge to defend a rabbit, let alone much of the land of Terrene. He was so far out of his league he felt completely overwhelmed. How could Grayson possibly entrust such a responsibility to him?

His parents' faces floated into his mind. They were alive and they would fight. They would expect no less from him. He squared his shoulders and his jaw. He would do the very best he could to live up to Grayson's and his parents' trust. That was all anyone could do.

He entered the living quarters resolved to be strong and fight to the end.

Commander Scarabee and Peter stood when he entered. Colin stopped in front of them and got straight to the point. He told them of Grayson's requests, and they didn't blink an eye. Peter had seen the resolve in Colin's eyes, but he was just a boy. "What of you, Colin?" he asked quietly.

Colin swallowed the lump in his throat but spoke with authority. "I will assist in any way I can. I will be able to follow your progress and will use anything within my power to vanquish the enemy and keep you and Terrene safe."

"And do you know the enemy?" he asked.

Colin blinked. "No, I do not. I will recognize them, however, when I see them. I am sure of it."

The Commander narrowed his eyes. "You will recognize them, lad, you will. Death Reapers from Hell they are, and they look the part." He nodded. "Yes, you will know them when they come."

"What of the dragons of the Cagars?" Peter asked. "You did not mention them."

"You know of the dragons?" Colin exclaimed. He walked closer to Peter, his face alight with excitement.

"Do *I know* them?" Peter chortled, digging his elbow into the hard shell of the Commander. "Yes, indeed. There won't be an unsinged stalk of vegetation left in Terrene if they get riled, so let's hope they throw all their fury at the Reapers."

Colin smiled. "Grayson said they will take care of themselves."

Peter agreed. "That they will. That they will. Good luck, boy wizard. God be with you and with all of us," he said, as he and the Commander vanished before Colin's startled eyes.

Grayson took his leave of Hernsart soon after talking with Colin. They had had word that Death Reapers were heading toward the border between the Gehenna and Fingal's Land. Grayson figured they would also try to storm through the Cliffs of the Ancient Cromlech, the Great Southern Plains, and the Valley of the Forgotten Abbey. They must be ready from every direction.

Hagan failed to talk him out of going, as did Aggie. He traveled on fleetfooted Celeritas into the Land of Frozen Waters. The great black war horse stood out in stark contrast to the snow and ice that made up the Land of Frozen

Waters. They rode hard toward the Ice Queen's castle where Simon awaited orders.

The alabaster castle was embedded into the hills some distance from the Northern Mountains. It was not just one structure but many, each connected to the other by swinging bridges between the giant evergreens which were almost always heavy with snow. It was a formidable fortress, able to be defended from every angle, not that its occupants had had to defend it in too many years to count. The walls that had been down all these many years, deep in the snowy earth, now were raised, and guards stood at the four entrances to the castle grounds.

The castle was known as the Ice Castle and the name did it justice. It was as white as the snow and the ice sculptures that swept the grounds and the lake beyond gave it the appearance of a fairy land – which indeed it is.

The Ice Queen was called Apricity. Her tower overlooked the Frozen Waters Lake. This magnificent body of water was artwork itself, translucent as glass, its icy patterns forming magnificent sculptures carved by mother nature herself. The artwork was so unusual that anyone walking along the iced-over surface of the lake would believe themselves in another world.

The lake was formed by the Abhanmohr River which flowed from the Crystal Mountains far to the west all the way across Fingal's Land and finally to the Frozen Waters Lake. Snowbirds by the hundreds flitted among the branches of the towering trees. Their singing awakened the castle's inhabitants every morning and eased them to sleep each night.

The land surrounding the castle is inhabited by a motley crew of every type of fairy known – alven, ashrays, brownies, clurichaun, water guardians, sprites, Will O'Wisp. Most fairies are as strong as humans, wise, telepathic, and able to heal any ailment, great or small, and these were no exception.

The great Elven nation built the magnificent castle, and it is testament to their skill and appreciation for everything beautiful and grand. These were the Grey Elves, reclusive protectors whose descendants continue to occupy the castle along with their Queen.

Their kin, the Noble Elves, call the tall peaks of the Northern Mountains their home. It is the most magnificent place in Terrene, filled with elegance and light. Rather than facing in towards the land, its main extension faces outward to the Sea of Mists, with its back turned towards the Land of Frozen Waters.

It allows the elves to keep watch in both directions. These elves are aristocratic warriors, who practice magic and speak in an ancient language only known to them and one other, though they can communicate with any person or creature. These are the elves of the secret train that runs along the northern and eastern borders of the Land of Frozen Waters through a hidden passage behind an arched bridge built many millennia ago.

Grayson was admitted through the heavy gate into the castle grounds and then made his way to the main castle door. The door was opened by an immaculate gray- haired elf who bade him enter. Grayson would not be relieved of his staff or his hat, but asked that his horse be taken care of. The elf nodded and led him to the great hall where Apricity and Simon sat drinking tea and eating cake. They both smiled broadly when Grayson entered the room. Simon jumped up. "Come join our party," he said, sweeping his hand to a seat at the table where fresh tea had just appeared, and where several of the small cakes still sat on a golden platter. Olcan lifted his massive head to acknowledge Grayson before laying it back down over his crossed paws. Grayson scratched his furry head.

Apricity remained seated as Grayson came to greet her. "Greetings, Your Majesty," he said with all the charm he could muster.

Apricity laughed as she placed her hand into his. It was an old joke between them. She was not called *Your Majesty* by anyone, preferring to be called by her name, as any other person would be called. Even Alexander, her so called butler, had finally adopted a more informal way of addressing her. He called her *My Lady* and would not budge from that.

She took in Grayson's haggard appearance as she greeted him. He would need rest and a good meal. She would see that he got both before he left. She smiled and pressed his hand before letting it go.

Grayson only relented to staying the night because it was late, and he wanted to see and talk to her and Simon, and because he knew he would function better if he had an uninterrupted rest and a full belly. The cooks at the castle were the best he had ever encountered, and he looked forward to anything they might place before him.

The next morning Grayson and Simon made their way on foot to the system of tunnels that ran underneath the Land of Frozen Waters, leaving Celeritas and Olcan in the Ice Queen's care. The tunnels ran north from the castle to the Northern Mountains, east to the Derryveaghs, and south to the Cliffs of the Ancient Cromlech. This gave Apricity and her people options in case of disaster. The tunnels were well fortified and could not be breached.

The latter direction was their destination and they traveled quickly, Grayson now regretting the lost time even though he felt much better for it.

Olcan had been ordered to stay behind, but he took orders – even from Grayson - only when he desired, and he thought this time it would be prudent to tag along, so padded softly into the tunnels behind them.

Grayson stood in the shadows of a slit-like opening high above the Gehenna. Simon stood on the other side of the opening squinting at the beehive of activity down below. Olcan came silently from the deeper shadows and sat beside Grayson, who looked upon the great beast and shook his head. He was not in the least surprised.

"There must be thousands of them," Simon whispered, aghast. No amount of imagining the worst had prepared him for the sight below.

Teeming masses of non-humanity marched toward Fingal's Land, towing with them huge platforms fitted with massive slings, battering rams, or spears placed a foot apart across the front of a large, wheeled wagon of sorts. The spears were at chest level and if the wagon was on any kind of incline, Simon couldn't imagine what havoc it would wreak on foot soldiers. It would also act as a shield for the soldiers following it. He shuddered at the thought of having to wage battle as a mere mortal man.

As they continued to watch, they heard rumbling sounds and were shocked to see three heavy conveyances of a type they'd never seen, roll forward, running under their own power! Simon's eyes met Grayson's.

"You will have to burn them," Grayson mouthed. Simon nodded. Those transports would have to be destroyed first, then the wagons. It would be his pleasure to be their destroyer.

Grayson was transfixed by it all. All of Terrene had been so happy in their peaceful lives, they had become lazy and complacent. Until the marauders had destroyed a couple of villages more recently, Terrene had not seen violence in too many years to count – since Grayson banished Ben Toreke into Hell if truth be told.

As Grayson stared at the horror below, he fixed on Ben Toreke. He had picked him out almost the minute he first looked below from the eye of the

Ancient Cromlech he now stood upon. The Death Reapers would not know what hit them when the Cromlech awoke. In fact, they had quite a few surprises in store for them. He chuckled soundlessly.

As they continued to watch, Ben Toreke looked up toward the very opening they stood in. The man apparently had an uncanny power for sniffing out his enemies. Aggie had warned Grayson of this, and he was prepared. Yet still the gruesome leader of the Death Reapers seemed to pick him out. How? He glanced over at Simon, moving nothing but his eyes, and then down at Olcan.

Olcan slowly backed deeper into the eye of the Cromlech. Olcan! Of course. He had been the one to disarm Toreke in another lifetime, which had allowed Grayson to fling him into the pits of Hell. His spell had not included Olcan because the huge wolf was supposed to be at the Ice Castle with Apricity.

Grayson motioned for Simon to move away from the opening. Olcan now crouched in the deepest shadows, a low, menacing growl deep in his throat. "Come, Olcan," Grayson whispered.

When they got to the far side of the Cromlech, Grayson spoke to Simon. "Don't try to handle those contraptions alone. I don't trust them to be what they appear. Get Greystone and Zephuros to join you. Toreke's Reapers are headed toward the border with Fingal's Land. Hagan should be nearing the Abhanmohr by now. Alfred will be advancing across Fingal's River. When those transports roll onto Fingal's Land and the battle begins, hit them with all you have and then retreat back to the mountain."

"I must hurry," Simon said as he readied himself to leap from the mountain. Grayson laid a hand on his arm, "Do not let Greystone and Zephuros get out of hand. They mean well but their fire could just as easily incinerate friend as well as foe."

Simon nodded and launched himself from the side of the craggy cliff and, as Grayson watched, metamorphosed into the magnificent Phantom of the Sky. "Godspeed, old friend," Grayson whispered.

He turned. "Olcan, you must go quickly to join the other wolves."

In answer, the behemoth stared back at Grayson and yawned, his huge mouth as large as a piskie's head. He stood four feet tall, was six feet long not counting his tail, and weighed close to twelve stone. He was the largest of the great timber wolves that inhabited the Cosmic Caverns Tundra. He wasn't going anywhere.

Grayson rolled his eyes and threw up his hands in mock exasperation. "Have it your way then, but keep up!" He headed down the steep face of the Cromlech he was standing on, to its shoulder far below. When he arrived, he pretended not to see Olcan there waiting for him. Instead, he went to gaze over the Land of Frozen Waters and whispered into the wind.

Then raising his hands toward the sky he spoke in a voice that thundered across the Cliffs.

Depart your sleep!
Oh, guardians of the Keep.
Awaken from your slumber
And join with our number
To defeat the mighty foe
As you promised long ago!

His words echoed back to him. "Awake! Awake!" he cried, drawing the words out and flinging them into the air.

He felt the reverberations beneath him and followed Olcan closer to the neck of the giant Cliff man. He nodded. The Cromlech would honor their commitment as he had known they would.

Grayson listened to the great groaning, creaking, grinding, as the boulders awoke. Grayson found himself enthralled by the massive creatures. They were cliffs while they slept, but when they awoke, though they were rooted to their spots, they could manipulate the mountain to do their bidding, causing landslides, earthquakes, and boulder sized hailstorms. They would be an unparalleled addition to the defense of the Land of Frozen Waters and the destruction of Toreke's stronghold.

He closed his eyes and spoke into the wind. It would deliver his message from one end of the Cliffs to the other.

Behold the enemy at Hell's Door
Cast them back into Terrene's Core
Back to the roar of the fire below
Back to damnation they must go.
Wait one day, not one day more
Then return them where they were before.

Grayson took in a long breath. He was exhausted. Olcan stood beside him, and he laid his hand on his furry head. "You must make your own way from here, my friend," he murmured fondly, as he was swooped up by Sky Strike. He must visit the Noble Elves.

Olcan watched their departure. In minutes he was on the Tundra. The wolves were ready to defend the land of the elves.

Chapter Twenty-Three

The Noble Elves knew of the calamity that had befallen the Gehenna, and of the darkness that would soon take over Terrene if the evildoers were not stopped. Arweinydd stood on a balcony high above the icy land below. He preferred not to interfere in wars, particularly those fought strictly for tyrannical purposes. This war, however, would be fought for the very lives of all that existed on Terrene and for Terrene itself. Still, he hesitated.

From his vantage point he could see the shimmering Ice Castle far away across the frozen landscape. It blended into the landscape flawlessly, but his eyes were sharper than any human eye, or animal eye, for that matter, and he could see it clearly.

His own home, high in the peaks of the Northern Mountains blended into the mountains as well. Elves had built them both and elven buildings were always constructed as an extension of nature. He noticed that Apricity had raised the castle's fortification walls, but still, it would be very rare indeed for anyone to pick out the castle from the hills and trees it was built into. Even the guards, standing motionless in their snowy outfits, could not be easily distinguished from the land.

He returned to the interior of his own fortress, if one could call it that. He sighed in appreciation of the graceful architecture and elegant furnishings surrounding him. Even deep in the mountains, his home was light and airy, sumptuous even.

The idea of war coming to such a peaceful place, undoing all the work that had taken generations to build, was unsettling. How had they allowed it to happen? Better still, how had Ben Toreke escaped from the bottomless firepit he had been cast into? How had he managed to build a formidable army right under their noses? He shook his head. This war wouldn't be easily fought. Or won. It would take all of Terrene's diverse population to defeat the evil creatures that threatened them.

The elves would do their part. Simon had already informed him of the danger, and he had agreed to join with the other elements of the country to defeat Toreke and his fiends. Even so, it lay heavy upon him. Elves could live hundreds, even thousands, of years. But they could succumb to wounds almost as easily as the other groups that called Terrene home. He would never ask his people to risk their longevity in normal times. But these were far from normal times. There was no other way. He would summon the council today. There would be no vote. He knew if he asked them to fight, they would.

He had walked the width of his mountain retreat, Glanymor, when he heard Grayson walking up the mountain from the abandoned aerie on the cliffs below. He called for tea and was standing in the wide alcove above the Sea of Mists when Grayson was announced.

Arweinydd turned to face his friend and smiled. "Sky Strike could have brought you closer," he greeted him.

Grayson cocked a brow at him. "Your hearing is still beyond measure, I see."

Arweinydd shook his head as he clasped Grayson's hand. He was a tall man, slim, with dark hair that reached below his shoulders and a face that showed maturity, but little sign of aging. "It is a plague at times to hear a leaf fall from a distant tree, but at least I can control it – to a point," he said wryly.

He motioned Grayson to a seat next to the tea service and a tray laden with treats. "I was expecting you today, so was listening for your step." He poured them both a cup of tea. "Try some of Altamore's bara brith. I fancy it is as good as that prepared by Apricity's cooks."

Grayson smiled around his cup of tea and reached for a slice of the tasty bread. He chewed thoughtfully. "It is at least as good."

Arweinydd laughed. "It is good to see you, Grayson." His laughter subsided. "Though I would naturally have preferred it to be under more pleasant circumstances." He set aside his tea and tented his hands under his chin almost as though he were praying. "The sea is the calmest I have seen it in ages," he remarked, reaching for a piece of bread and settling back into his chair. "The calm before the storm is not a myth, you know," he said quietly.

"Yes, I know," Grayson answered. "I, too, feel the storm approaching." They both knew they were not speaking of a storm caused by nature – the mountains protected them from the worst of that type of storm. They spoke of the storm brewing in Gehenna that could destroy their entire world.

They were silent, each with his own thoughts, chewing the tasty bread and drinking the strong, honey sweetened tea. After swallowing his last morsel of the bara brith, Grayson said, "You must summon the bridge."

Arweinydd leaned forward and sighed. "Yes." He lowered his voice, not because he was afraid of spies among the elves. They were all honest, trustworthy, and kind. But because he wanted no one, not even his closest confidants to believe he might think this war would end badly for them. He *didn't* think that, not really, but was a cautious man. Every precaution must be taken.

"I will move the trains to every conceivable track in the mountains. That will still leave a few places lacking, however. I have made additions, but it is not wise to place even enchanted trains where evil hands may claim them. Who knows what powers Toreke may possess to have escaped from such a fiery inferno as Hell?" He shook his head. "Thankfully, the trains cannot be activated by any enemy, so even if Toreke's men gain access to the caverns they will not be able to activate the trains." He grimaced. "I hope."

Arweinydd continued, "You must relay to all of your leaders to take their troops to the mountains if they are over-run. They need to know no more. Even those that are among Terrene's people will not be able to board the train if they are untrustworthy. The trains will be able to tell, and they will be barred."

The two great leaders sat in brooding silence. War was not something either wanted. But both would fight to the death to defend Terrene. If things did not go their way, there was only one escape. The trains would speed across the great arched bridge to the seaworthy vessels hidden in the bay below Glanymor. No one knew of the existence of the trains, the bridge, or the ships but the two men seated at the table.

Grayson huffed a breath and stood. "Well, on that note, I believe I will take your last slice of bread and depart for Hernsart.".

Arweinydd awoke from his thoughts. "Two things before you go. There is a man named McBride who has amassed a number of followers. He has been seen more than once inside the Gehenna talking to Ben Toreke."

Grayson's brows shot up. "A traitor in our midst?" he asked under his breath. "I know that man. He lived in Nil's Knob and traveled as far as Fir Bolg with Lucas and Aggie when they led the villagers to Bodun. Alfred must be informed at once!"

Arweinydd agreed. "Yes. The sooner the better. McBride and his men will either try to sabotage Alfred's forces, or they will have already joined Toreke's

Death Reapers. Toreke may already be privy to Alfred's plans and that will not play out well."

"I must go," Grayson said, heading for the door he had entered not so long ago.

"Wait," Arweinydd called. "Come with me. The train will get you to Hernsart – and Quant – much quicker."

As they strode from the room, Grayson looked at the tall, noble elf beside him. One would never think that beneath his genteel look and courtly manner breathed one of the fiercest warriors the world would ever know.

Arweinydd stopped Grayson inside the tunnel where the golden train awaited. "One more thing. You must know how to summon the bridge."

Grayson stared at him as though he had lost his mind. "Perhaps you should entrust one of your own people with that knowledge, though I pray it will never be needed. You are a fierce warrior. You will surely live to summon the bridge yourself."

"We cannot take that chance." He leaned into Grayson's ear and whispered the secret code.

Grayson smiled. "I believe I can remember that."

He clasped Arweinydd's hand. "Until we meet again," he said gravely as he stepped aboard the enchanted train and was whisked west toward the Cosmic Caverns. Quant would be there, even though Hagan and his troops were on the move. He would have to summon Celeritas, and he would have to see that Alfred was notified of McBride's treason.

Arweinydd watched the train out of sight. "Until we meet again," he whispered.

Chapter Twenty-Four

Colin, dressed in his new cloak, dagger at his waist, pentacle in place around his neck, and his staff and wand close by, gently stirred the water in the cauldron, then stood watching as the ripples faded and the translucent water stilled. He could summon visions by focusing his mind on what he was trying to conjure. At present he was attempting to visualize the fighting friars of the Forgotten Abbey - more out of curiosity than need - and wasn't sure it was within his capabilities. They would certainly need no help from him, but he was curious about what they were doing.

He could not get a huge visual that would show the entire abbey or all the friars, but even a sliver of something might give him the information he wanted. As he watched the water settle, he saw a section of a craggy mountain with what seemed to be a sheer face pocked with crevices. As he bent to peer closely at the small section of mountainside that was visible, he saw a man dressed in full battle regalia and holding one of the staff-like sticks he had seen the monks practice their fighting with. He wore a shield and had a short sword strapped to his hip. Rather than red garments, the man seemed to be clothed entirely in gray, a gray the same color as the precipice he was standing on. His head was covered with a cap, or perhaps the hood of his shirt, that placed his face in shadow, and he hadn't moved so much as an eyelash that Colin could tell since he first set eyes on him. He couldn't see any more details but knew from the little he saw that the man was awaiting the call for battle. Colin surmised that the entire mountainside was covered with other such men, but of course, had no way of knowing. Perhaps the lone man was a scout?

Colin left the water and went to stand in front of the large map of Terrene. He found the Valley of the Forgotten Abbey easily. Since he had surmised that the friar he saw was a guard or scout, he most likely was concealed on the northern side of the Omoud Range, low mountains that ran from the Derryveaghs to the Misty Mountains and divided the land of the Gehenna from the Valley of the Forgotten Abbey. Colin noticed that a wide chasm or gorge splayed out from the mountains. This chasm and the steep mountains would make it doubly difficult for an attack to come to the Abbey from the Gehenna.

Would the Abbey even *need* to be defended? And, if not, would Abbot Tomas involve them in the fight at all? Was there a way to attack across the chasm, or would they merely stand their ground and prevent anyone from crossing over to the mountains?

Colin bowed his head in thought. On the one hand, he would never wish anyone harm by joining in the fight, but on the other hand, Terrene would need every able-bodied fighter to defend it. The fighting might of the Abbey could throw the balance either way. What should he do? What *could* he do?

He was so lost in thought that he didn't notice a small green mass that looked like a large rock uncurl itself and sit up, blinking in the light. A slight noise startled Colin, however, and he gasped as he saw the diminutive dragon looking at him with bold emerald-green eyes and a skeptical look on his face.

"You're not very observant, are you?" the dragon asked, startling Colin even more.

" What are you doing here?" Colin asked, his voice going high at the end.

The small dragon huffed. "I live here, of course."

"That can't be," Colin said firmly. "I would have seen you before if you lived here."

"Well, you're obviously not very observant," the maddening dragon announced. "And besides, you wouldn't ever see me if I didn't allow it to be so."

Colin stared at him. "Whoever you are, and wherever you came from, you need to leave. You are not allowed here. And, besides, I don't believe you live here."

The dragon sighed, as if dealing with such a dunce as Colin took all his energy. "I didn't mean I live here as in this room. I meant that I live here as in this mountain."

Colin closed his eyes and shook his head vigorously, hoping to rid himself of any illusion that a green-scaled, green-eyed, irritable, talking dragon had gained entrance to the Enchantment Room. It wasn't possible.

When he opened his eyes, the dragon was still there. "Bother!" he exhaled. How did he get in? Colin quickly glanced around the room. Doors and windows were secured, as they should be.

"Don't worry," Green-eyes – for that was what Colin decided to call him, if he had to call him at all - piped up. "You're not losing your mind." *Though you wouldn't have far to go,* he smirked to himself. "I came through the walls. Don't you know anything about the Dragons of the Cagars?"

Colin's eyes widened. "Did you say the dra-dragons of the Cagars?" he stammered. He had certainly not thought the great dragons of the Cagars would be such pip-squeaks. He had envisioned thousands of Phantoms, not small green dragons that talked way too much and broke into places they had no business being.

Green-eyes rolled his eyes. "You hard of hearing, too?"

"N-no," Colin replied.

"Well then, listen up. I am a dragon of the Cagars." He enunciated each word slowly as if speaking to someone who was addle-brained or worse.

Colin snorted and drew himself up as far as he could stretch to make himself look taller. He narrowed his eyes at the small dragon. "And *I* am Colin Ceartas of Nil's Knob, now of Fearann Draoidh. I am a wizard and Assistant to Grayson Ghlic, Guardian of Terrene. And you, *Green-eyes*, are trying my patience," he announced in his most Grayson-like tone.

The dragon pretended to shiver in fright, then grinned, his small sharp teeth gleaming. "Well, I'll be. You have a modicum of spunk, it seems." He looked Colin up and down before clambering onto the table, scattering papers to the floor. Ignoring the fallen papers, he sat down on the cleared off space on the table.

"The Dragons of the Cagars have been here since the beginning of time," he began. "You have never seen us because no one will ever see us unless we wish them to – like now. We come and go as we please and most of the time it pleases us to stay in our side of the mountains. We do not meddle in anyone's business, and they don't meddle in ours." He stared at Colin, like a professor totally unimpressed by his pupil.

"However," he droned on, "war will be upon us in hours. We will defend these mountains until our last drop of blood has seeped out onto the stones. We are not big, but we are mighty. Have no doubt about that!" His eyes flashed, daring Colin to comment.

Colin took a deep breath and sank into the chair near the fearsome dragon. For he was indeed fearsome when his viridescent eyes glared daggers, and passion reverberated from every inch of his body.

Colin took a calming breath. He and Green-eyes had gotten off on the wrong foot, and that would not do. Grayson had spoken well of the Dragons of the Cagars, and he might need their help. Making a decision, he said, "Grayson trusts you implicitly, and because he is a wise and valiant man, then so shall I." He fidgeted before blurting out a question that had been on his mind. "What of Phantom of the Sky?"

The dragon looked perplexed. "Phantom? What about him?"

Colin rubbed his nose. "Well, I . . ." What exactly was he asking? It would be rude to ask how such tiny midget dragons came to share the Cagars with the giant warrior dragon, Phantom of the Sky. He was afraid Green-eyes would be offended and think he was belittling him. Ha! Be*littling*. That was funny.

He cleared his throat and began again. "Well, I was just wondering what the Cagar dragons' relationship might be to Phantom of the Sky since you apparently share the same space?"

Green-eyes scoffed. "Phantom and Simon are an atypical phenomenon – not an everyday kind of relationship, you know. Besides the fact that we are all dragons, the only thing we have in common is Grayson."

He smiled slyly before saying, "Grayson is a dragon master, a wizard that protects dragons and is exceedingly wise in the ways of dragons. Not only us and Phantom, but the ferocious dragons of the Land of Frozen Waters." He flicked his tail and sent the rest of the papers tumbling to the floor. "Bu-u-u-t," he dragged the word out, "Grayson does not *profess* to be a dragon master. In this realm, we are all protectors of each other."

Colin nodded. He could see the benefit of that, and that Grayson would not want the power that he possessed to be thought better, or controlling, of others. Dragons that could walk through walls, fly (for Green-eyes had wings that he folded around himself like a cloak), and were as intelligent (though irritating) as this one was, could surely offer assistance to Grayson. Protection, he wasn't so sure. Colin knew little of dragons but did know they were imbued with magical powers. One thing he had learned, though, from Green-eyes was rather curious. Simon was the only human that could morph into a dragon. It still puzzled him whether Phantom could be called a real dragon if he was also a human. He shook his head. He had no idea how all that worked.

He bent to pick up the scattered papers. "So why have you come to the Enchantment Room?" he asked as he placed the papers in a safer place underneath a vivid, blue-flecked stone.

Green-eyes narrowed his eyes to slits and wagged his head. "I have been given the dubious honor of protecting you."

Colin's head jerked up. "I don't need protecting by some half grown, irritable . . ."

"Save your voice," Green-eyes interrupted. "It will only be wasted." He peered at Colin. "Know that the orders have been given; they will not be revoked. You might order me away, but could you ever be sure I left? Hmm-m-m-m?" He answered his own question as Colin's face darkened. "No, you could not. I will remain here wandering around wherever you go. The only question is: Do you want to wonder where I am and what I might be up to? Or do you want to be able to see me so you'll know for sure?" He asked smugly.

Colin dropped his head into his hands. Not much of a choice, it seemed. He jumped to his feet. "If you have to be here you need to get off that table. That's my workspace." They glared at each other for a moment before Green-eyes jumped agilely down onto the chair and then to the floor and went to curl up underneath the apothecary table. Before his bright eyes closed, he said, "We are one thousand strong. Fearann Draoidh will never fall, you may rest assured."

Colin bent to his task, setting everything he might need in a hurry on the tabletop in precise order. He separated the papers and placed them in a line behind the objects he had lined up. He chose several potion bottles, mixed the potions, and placed them at the end of his line of materials. He then stood back and studied them. They would do for now.

He went to stand over the cauldron and rippled the water with his hand. Unbidden, a view of Olcan surfaced. The giant timber wolf was charging towards something, hackles raised, teeth bared.

Chapter Twenty-Five

War came to Terrene and was just as horrific, violent, chilling, bleak, destructive, and disheartening as war always is.

Battles were fought in Fingal's Land, across the Great Southern Plains, in the Land of Frozen Waters, and in the Gehenna itself, where the original Gehenna people were freed by the fighting friars and fought side by side with their liberators to reclaim their homeland (such as it is). They had been rounded up by Ben Toreke and put to work in the caves mining the metals that would be used to make their weapons. They were incredibly happy to have their revenge. The Gehenna people and the friars would never be friends – they had nothing in common – but they could be allies for a common cause. They were fierce and independent and lived harsh, hardscrabble lives, but if they were content with that barren land, who are we to try to convince them otherwise?

The Cromlech held their Cliffs effortlessly, creating chaos amongst the Death Reapers and banishing any who showed his terrible visage back to Hell where he belonged. At the end of the war, Hell's Door was closed permanently with stones from the Cromlech, and a spell that could never be broken.

The Death Reapers and their deadly machines flowed over the Gehenna border into Fingal's Land, the Great Southern Plains, and the Land of Frozen Waters like raging ants, thousands of them bent on destruction. They were not long in the Land of Frozen Waters because the Noble Elves, led by Arweinydd, and the Grey Elves and fairies, led by their Queen, along with the mighty dragons and the magnificent birds of prey made short shrift of them before much damage was done. The bodies of the Reapers lay sprawled over the southwestern corner of that frozen land but, having no blood, their deaths did not mar the landscape. Instead, their bodies disintegrated into millions of pieces and were swept away by the wind across the mountains and back through Hell's Door into the fiery furnace below.

The great fortress of Hernsart was wrecked before Phantom, Greystone, and Zephuros could destroy all of the lethal machines, but in the end enough was left that it could be re-built. In the meantime, the elderly, women who were not Defenders, and the children of Hernsart could remain in the mountain caverns above the Cosmic Caverns Tundra where they had waited out the war.

The piskies, true to their word, tricked the Isnana into the spider holes above the Gehenna and as they dropped from the sky near the Cauldron, they devoured everything in their path, including many horrified Reapers, some jumping into the boiling Cauldron to escape the massive monsters.

The spell cast on the Isnana by the piskies lasted only for one day, but that day was interminable for the Death Reapers who had been left to stoke the fires and pile the weapons for the Reapers who fought in battle. The Isnana disappeared back into the spider holes as quickly as they had appeared, leaving a path of destruction that was unimaginable to those that had not witnessed it firsthand.

The piskies rode into battle on the backs of the flying Ceffyl Dwrs, horses that inhabited the cold waters of the Blue River. The Ceffyl Dwr were as mischievous as the piskies, so the two were evenly matched. They were known to dissolve into mist at a moment's notice, sometimes dropping an unwary rider to his death. The people of Terrene had learned long ago to avoid them, but the piskies had an understanding with the elusive creatures. They provided them with the strawberries, small pumpkins, pineapple, and the wild watermelon that they craved in exchange for allowing the piskies to ride them. This partnership had lasted as long as memory and would continue until the Ceffyl Dwr lost their taste for the sweet fruits - which was highly unlikely.

Together they were like murderous hornets on the battlefield, zooming in to attack, with the piskies stabbing with their poison-laced sharp spears and flinging poisonous potions over the heads of the Death Reapers while the tenacious Ceffyl Dwr wielded their razor hooves and barbed teeth to deadly advantage. Because they attacked from the air, they were a distraction to the Reapers who were engaged in battle on the ground. Apparently, Ben Toreke was the only Reaper that could fly.

They were not the only distraction. The fierce dragons of the north, Phantom, Zephuros, and Greystone attacked the deadly machines of the Reapers with a vengeance, but sadly, not before one of them came within range of Hernsart. Troops had been sent to the Abhanmohr to quell the attack, but Ben Toreke had outmaneuvered them and had sent a contingent of men with one of the machines, which was equipped with a type of sled that sped easily over the southwestern corner of the snowy Land of Frozen Waters. They had bypassed the battle that had raged nearby, and under cover of darkness had reached Fingal's Land and then Hernsart. Phantom managed to get to the area in time to destroy the machine, but not before Hernsart had suffered significant damage.

The Reapers fighting between the Abhanmohr and the Plains were further distracted by hundreds of fierce gnomes who exploded from the ground underneath their feet, chopping off legs and shattering bones with their grisly axes and hammers.

In the Great Southern Plains, Peter's Windwalkers, with their neeston riders, sailed through the Reapers, biting and kicking while the neeston spewed mists of noxious, disorienting smoke over them. The Specter panthers, invisible like the neeston, attacked the enemy at will. The Reapers were dead without ever knowing what got them.

Commander Scarabee's troops transformed into vicious giant insects which could fight from the air, or stand on their back legs and wield weapons in their four remaining legs. They were a gruesome sight, but brave fighters. When outnumbered, they emitted a toxic fume that caused the Reapers to turn and flee right into the jaws of the panthers or into the paths of other defenders of Terrene.

Colin watched in amazement and a great degree of pride as the Dragons of the Cagar shot exploding balls of fire from their mouths with such accuracy he saw no target unscathed. When the thousand strong green dragons joined the battle, only Green-eyes remained behind. He was there to protect Colin, and though he felt he would have loved the rush of battle, he was adamant in his refusal to budge from Colin's side.

Truthfully, though, Colin was in no danger. Grayson had sealed the magical mountain around him. The battle came a wee bit closer than Grayson would have liked, however. The traitor, McBride, and the few traitorous men that followed him, appeared back in Nil's Knob as the battle raged and the Death Reapers began to fail at their mission of destroying every living creature on Terrene.

A troop of Defenders closed in on McBride's trail before it was cold, having been sent by Alfred to apprehend the scoundrels. Colin strained his eyes seeking his parents among the Defenders, but no matter how much he wished it, they were not there. He did see that McBride had laid a hasty trap for the Defenders, and it gave him immense pleasure and not a little satisfaction to blow their plans to smithereens with a well-placed spell and several helpful explosions from Green-eyes, who vacated his spot beside Colin just long enough to fly close enough that his explosions would hit their targets.

The Defenders were startled by the explosions, but not as much as they would have been if McBride's scheme had worked. They rallied quickly and captured McBride and two of his men; the others having been killed in the blast.

Far away across Fingal's Land, Aggie and Lucas fought with a large contingent of Defenders from Hernsart, across the Abhanmohr and to the border of the Gehenna. They were sent to destroy any weapons and any Reapers that remained inside the Gehenna lands. They had covered the land between the Misty Mountains and the Sliabh Dearg without incident, and had just reached the top of the Sliabh Dearg when the Isnana fell from the sky. Aggie was just as shocked as she had thought she would be to see the horrific giant spiders spinning down from the spider holes, plowing through everything that stood in their way, their massive jaws destroying anything in their path. Luckily, the destruction took place in the land around the cauldron, and not as far west as the mesa they stood upon.

The Defenders stood silent, repelled by the slaughter and destruction, but having the good sense to stay well back from the chaos that ensued below. Some of the Reapers ran headlong into the Cauldron to avoid the spiders. Either way they were dead, and who can say which death would have been preferable?

The Defenders watched as the spiders picked the area around the Cauldron completely clean before spinning back into the holes above and disappearing. The Defenders then turned back towards Fingal's Land. Their job had been done for them and for that they were grateful, though the war was far from over.

As Aggie descended from the Misty Mountains, she stared towards the Fearann Draiodh. "We are coming, Colin," she whispered. She and Lucas exchanged a look. They would see their son soon. They knew it.

Chapter Twenty-Six

Grayson had fought alongside Hagan's men from Hernsart to the Abhanmohr before joining the fray in the Land of Frozen Waters. Once the fighting there was done and Hagan's men turned back towards Fingal's Land, he was exhausted and sought refuge at the Ice Queen's castle. He would need to rest and summon all of the energy he possessed before he took on Toreke, for take him on he would have to do.

It was quiet at the castle, for most of the elves and fairies were guarding the perimeters of their land, including the Cliffs, the tunnels, and the barricade within the Derryveaghs that had been erected to prevent any Reaper from gaining access to the Land of Frozen Waters through the mountains. Grayson smiled grimly. Best laid plans and all that. No matter, there was always something that could go wrong.

As Grayson approached, the gate swung open and the Ice Queen herself welcomed him. Grayson smiled and tried to hide his weariness, but Apricity was not fooled.

"You look awful," she greeted him.

He knew he was a sight. He was grimy with ground in dirt on his body and in his clothes, his hair tangled around his shoulders, deep wrinkles showing in his face. There wasn't an inch of his body that didn't ache. Even so, he laughed, Apricity joining in.

"Come," she said, motioning for the guard to secure the gate as she led Grayson to a much needed bath and change of clothes.

After soaking in the warm water and then dressing in the soft clothes Apricity had left for him, he felt a little of the weariness fade away. He joined Apricity in front of a low fire in her quarters overlooking the Frozen Waters Lake. Their meal was already set out for them, and Grayson ate well for the first time in long days. They did not talk of war, but of other things, better days, and a future without the threat of war. Apricity was well aware that Grayson must defeat Ben Toreke before that future could become reality, for no one else had the power to do it. It must surely weigh heavily on his shoulders.

Grayson was fighting to stay awake as dessert was served, and after just a few bites, Apricity shook her head. "I see my charms have failed miserably tonight. You must go and rest, else your head will be in your pudding," she prodded him.

"I am the poor company, not you," Grayson said gallantly. "You are as charming as ever, but I believe you are right. My thoughts are completely muddled, and I do need sleep." He took her hand and smiled. "Goodnight, and thank you for providing shelter and sustenance for an old man."

"Pfft-t-t." Apricity retorted. "You're not an old man and you know it." She kissed his cheek and sent him to his bed, gazing at his retreating back thoughtfully.

When she could see him no more, she turned and went to stand at her windows, staring out at the frozen lake. It was dark, with only a half moon above, but the icy sculptures glittered. She would locate Ben Toreke and summon those that could help Grayson defeat that monster. She had no doubt that Grayson could defeat Toreke, but at what cost? She wasn't willing to chance it. He would not face Toreke alone if she had anything to say about it – and she did.

Grayson strode across the rocky summit of the highest peak of the Misty Mountains, his freshly washed and pressed cloak billowing in the wind, his face determined and set. Fog swirled over the lonely mountaintop, shrouding it in an eerie silence. He found Toreke high on a ledge overlooking the raging battle below. He was almost concealed as the mist eddied and flowed around him.

"I could have killed you many times on your way up the mountain, Wizard," Toreke rasped, as he turned. "But I prefer to kill you face to face." His maniacal laugh shattered the silence - until it stopped as suddenly as it had started. "Or should I say face to *no face*?" he mocked Grayson, throwing back his hood to reveal his shredded, moldering face, eyes like red embers.

"You did this to me, Wizard, and I shall enjoy my revenge as I destroy first you and then everything that you hold dear! Your mighty Terrene will be no more," he spat.

Grayson narrowed his eyes as a dozen Reapers stepped from their hiding places. "Not up to the task alone, I see," he derided Toreke.

Toreke smiled a ghastly smile, his eye sockets glowing red. "A little extra caution never hurt anyone," he taunted. "Looks like you could've used a little more foresight yourself."

Grayson continued to stare at Toreke's hideous face, not moving or changing expression, but feeling the Reapers creeping closer until they were stayed by a motion from Toreke. He would need every ounce of stamina and cunning he possessed. He tightened his grip on his staff, dimming the bright glow from the crystal embedded in it, and cleared his mind of everything but the macabre countenance of Ben Toreke. Drawing a deep breath and letting it out slowly, he faced his deadly foe. The fog would be his friend, for he could see through it. But could Toreke? Grayson had no way of knowing what new powers Toreke now held, but it mattered not. For Grayson must fight him to the death.

Toreke's ruthless eyes bored into Grayson as he advanced a few feet closer. "Are you ready to die?" he asked menacingly.

A voice answered from the gloom. "He is not the one to die this day, vile creature!"

Apricity. Grayson froze. What was she doing here? His eyes remained steadily on Toreke as he took in this new development.

"Tut, tut, pretty lady," Toreke taunted. He placed the sword he was carrying over what would have been his heart in a prior life. "We," he swung his sword around to include the Reapers gathered at his side, "are already dead. You must know that dead people cannot be killed." His smile was a grimace. "We cannot die but once."

Apricity snorted. She herself had sent many of the Death Reapers to their second death in the battle in her frozen land.

Tilting his head in Apricity's direction, he said, "As much as it wounds me, you have made your choice. You will have to join the Wizard in death. Perhaps in death, you will join me?"

Apricity stood as still as a pillar, not acknowledging Toreke in any way. As she saw Toreke's eyes widen for a split second, she smiled. She and Grayson were not alone. For as the fog lifted, Toreke could see that Arweinydd and Simon stood by her side. They came to stand with Grayson, Simon at his back and Apricity and Arweinydd on each side.

"This is not your fight," Grayson said, his eyes never leaving Toreke.

"It is as much ours, as it is yours," Arweinydd replied.

The melee, when it came, was brutal. One by one the Death Reapers were over-powered as Toreke stood by. He was astonished as each was definitively dispatched, their remains disintegrating, the tiny bits blown into the wind and straight to Hell's Door.

Finally, only Toreke was left. Grayson told Arwenydd, Simon, and Apricity to stand down. He would finish this himself.

Gathering his energy, Grayson sent a ball of fire straight toward Toreke's chest, but Toreke managed to sidestep just in time.

Grayson pounded his staff onto the ground, causing the rocks around Toreke's feet to shatter. Amazingly, Toreke sailed away from the shattering rocks and landed close enough to Grayson to strike at him with his sword. Grayson used his staff to block the sword, but not before receiving a minor cut. He muttered a curse and sent Toreke flying backwards, falling hard. The battle raged over the mountaintop until Toreke was hurled backwards and fell once more.

He jumped to his feet and threw his sword, surprising Grayson, who lunged to the side as the sword flew by his head. Toreke now held a strange object in his hand. As Grayson watched, Toreke pressed down on the object. Grayson quickly muttered an incantation to shield himself and the others as tiny sword-like objects whizzed through the air, exploding on contact with anything they hit. The shield held but was so battered by the barrage, it began to rip. Apricity used her powers to repair the shield, but they must do something to stop Toreke. If he had a limitless supply of these tiny explosives, they would be forced to go on the defensive.

As all their minds were focused on how best to proceed, Quant arrived and attacked Toreke from the air as Olcan charged from behind, knocking him sprawling and then pinning him to the ground. Quant caught the strange object neatly in his talons as it tumbled from Toreke's grasp, and flew away with it. Grayson swiftly dismantled the shield, and motioning the others to stay put, ran towards where Olcan had Toreke pinned to the ground. With a mighty thrust, Toreke loosened himself from the canine's grip. His arm, held tight in Olcan's massive jaws, was ripped from his body. As Toreke swayed on his feet, he let out a blood curdling scream. Grayson reached him as an army of Reapers tore up the mountainside towards them.

Everything was a blur after that. The fray that resulted from Toreke's screech for help not only brought the hordes of Reapers that had been fighting below, but also the Terrene defenders. The battle being fought in the valley moved as one forcefully up the mountain until gnomes were bursting from the ground, Defenders and their armies were overtaking Reapers and dispatching them back to Hell, Peter's Windwalkers and the neeston were trampling the repulsive creatures as they ran to the defense of their gory leader. The tides of battle changed significantly because the Reapers forgot everything as they ran to the aid of mighty Toreke. All of the very unique warriors of Terrene fought valiantly. Bravely. And after what seemed like hours, but in reality was not nearly so long, the Reapers were routed. When they died, they disintegrated and were moved by the wind back to their original burial place in the fiery pits of Hell.

Meanwhile, Toreke was surrounded by the best fighters in his forces until one by one they were killed, and disintegrated as their brethren had. As Toreke lay mortally wounded, a dark faced, white clad man walked onto the battlefield. Olcan, who had been about to shred Toreke's body into a thousand pieces, suddenly stopped, stood still, and sniffed the wind. Then with a glance at Grayson, sat down next to the fallen man. Grayson was baffled and said, "Finish the job, Olcan. We cannot be free until Toreke is dead and his body scattered." Olcan yawned, baring his teeth. Not at Grayson, but just as a warning to anyone else not to interfere.

Chapter Twenty-Seven

It was then that Grayson noticed the man approaching. Everything and everyone stilled as the man walked steadily to Toreke. Once there, he spat on the fallen man and waved his hands slowly over Toreke as he spouted words only Grayson and Arweinydd understood. Perhaps Toreke understood for fear sprang into his eyes as he lay writhing on the ground seemingly trying to get away from the man. Olcan watched him for a moment until he realized he was too far gone to make good his escape. The white clad man knelt beside Toreke, removed a silver dagger from its sheath and plunged it into the brain of the horrified Reaper, who drew a shuddering breath and lay still. The man removed the dagger and plunged it into the cavity where a heart should beat and left it there. As the onlookers watched, Ben Toreke began to shrivel until he would easily fit into two hands cupped together. The knife remained in the tiny bit of flesh remaining. The man turned to Grayson and spoke to him in the language he had used before.

"This ruthless tyrant will never threaten Terrene again. Do not return him to Hell. He must be buried with the dagger still in his chest inside an elven box filled with rainbow stones, fiery opals, and amethysts. Bury him inside the box in the deepest depths of the Sea. He has tried to destroy Gehenna and has slaughtered many of my people. We wish to remain as we were. We do not seek anything from the rest of Terrene." With that, he turned and began to thread his way back across the mountaintop toward Gehenna, that arid, hostile environment that he called home. He had only taken a few steps when Grayson called to him and spoke to him quietly; then looked after him until he was lost to sight. *The Wisdom-Keeper. How did he come to be here?* Grayson shook his head.

When Toreke died, the remaining Death Reapers all over Terrene quickly disintegrated into a vast storm of windblown fragments whirling like a monster tornado straight into Hell where they belonged. It took the Defenders of Terrene by surprise – one moment they were fighting for their lives and the life of Terrene and at the next moment the enemy disintegrated right in front of them. The number of Death Reapers was so great that the sky darkened as their fragments were blown toward Hell's Door.

Apricity, Arweinydd, and Grayson were waiting beside the gateway into Hell as the fragments spiraled downwards into the fiery pit. Each of them cast a spell that would close Hell's Door, and the Cliffs of the Ancient Cromlech sent hundreds of tons of stone crashing down to seal it forever.

Ben Toreke was deposited without ceremony into the Sea of Mists following the instructions of the old Gehenna leader. Grayson assured the others that the old man was quite versed in burial magic and demons, and they had no reason to question him further. The tale of the Wisdom-Keeper would make a good story for another day, Grayson thought, but not today. The Wisdom-Keeper had told Grayson that the marauders were his own people, captured early and forced to do Toreke's bidding in hopes that Toreke would allow their families to live. "They will not be punished," he said, his black eyes boring into Grayson's. "I was not there to save them."

In time, the dead of Terrene were buried, the injured healed. Families grieved, but there was much work to do. The towns and fortresses must be re-built. The trains were sent into seclusion once more. All of the creatures that had come together to fight for Terrene's survival, finally returned to their homes. Terrene's wounds were covered with new growth, grasses, trees, and flowers.

Lucas and Aggie returned to Nil's Knob. Colin returned with them for a long visit, but his place was with Grayson on Fearann Draoidh and they all knew it. Colin and Aggie could always communicate with their minds. From time to time, Colin would appear inside their home or beside them in their wanderings and they would soak up all the joy and love they could, for they could not know when they would meet again.

Life went on for the inhabitants of Terrene. And if they kept a closer watch on each other, who would blame them? If they stood more often on the perimeters of their lands and looked across the expanse, smelled the wind, and sighed, it was to be expected. They had let down their guard once. It would not happen again.

Grayson and the Wisdom-Keeper of Gehenna, whose name was Daniel, formed a relationship of sorts, wary at first, but as the years passed, that wariness turned to trust. Phantom of the Sky, or the great eagle, Sky Strike, flew over the Gehenna lands often, keeping watch. Sometimes a gray robed wizard was aboard. He would raise his staff to Daniel, and the old man would lift his eyes up, a rueful smile playing at his lips, and nod. In the absence of the Death Reapers, much of the darkness, acrid odors, and fiery skies had receded from the Gehenna, though it remained a desolate, arid place.

Grayson visited all the kingdoms in Terrene more often now and reveled in the lives of all its citizens. The fact that he could visit them all at the same time would've made it easier, but he preferred to use multilocation minimally. It was a tiring process, and to be truthful, he was getting too old for it.

As Colin continued to grow in stature and in power, Grayson occasionally left the mountain in his care and would head to the Land of Frozen Waters. He would knock at the door of Apricity's castle and, more often than not, be welcomed by Apricity herself. She would smile up at him, wind her arm through his, and together they would walk her icy kingdom, catching up with each other and planning a future for themselves and Terrene that was just, safe, and happy for all its inhabitants.

Together they visited Arweinydd, three old friends talking, sharing, eating, and laughing. The evil days were over – they hoped - and they flourished in each other's presence. But who could blame him if Grayson's eyes occasionally strayed to the crystal on his staff? Terrene was his home, and he would not be caught short again. He knew that any threat would not come from Ben Toreke or his Death Reapers the next time, but there was always a chance, no matter how small, that threats would come from yet unknown enemies. He and the wise leaders of Terrene would be ready.

Also by Reita O'Neal Jackson

Easy Street
The Defenders